Critical acclaim

'With his firmly rooted fr...
the most beguilingly repul...
Burgess's Enderby came to life in a Hove bedroom with
"a posterior riposte"'

Christopher Hawtree, *Independent*

'Impeccably researched and shows a great love of Britain
. . . this is a book with metaphysical ambition and
intellectual clout that is scarcely imaginable from any of
Lang's British contemporaries'

Stuart Jeffries, *Guardian*

'Weirdly compelling'   *The Times*

'Dark, disgustingly earthy, rich and funny'
Toby Clements, *Daily Telegraph*

Luc Lang was born in 1956. He lives in Paris.

Strange Ways

LUC LANG

Translated by
Rory Mulholland

PHOENIX

A PHOENIX PAPERBACK

First published in Great Britain in 2000
by Phoenix House
This paperback edition published in 2002
by Phoenix,
an imprint of Orion Books Ltd,
Orion House, 5 Upper St Martin's Lane,
London WC2H 9EA

First published in France in 1998
by Librairie Arthème Fayard
as *Mille six cents ventres*

Copyright © Librairie Arthème Fayard, 1998
English translation copyright © Rory Mulholland, 2000

A CIP catalogue record for this book
is available from the British Library.

ISBN 0 75381 413 7

Printed and bound in Great Britain by
Clays Ltd, St Ives plc

For Dagmar Rolf

Chapter 1

When I felt her hands kneading the nape of my neck and tousling my hair, when I looked at the quivering white bosom she offered me and the face that said no with such energy that her glasses flew off her nose and disappeared into the folds of the aniseed green sofa, I realized that here, between Louise's bare thighs, I had found a last wellspring of youth. God knows how I hate anyone ruffling the wave in my hair, the wave I so patiently restore each morning, but I looked at her face – cheeks pink, eyes closed, lips in a forgotten smile – her face that lay so close to mine, and I said nothing. 'The heart has no age,' my mother always tells me from the lofty heights of her eighty-seven years, to which I always retort: 'It's not what's inside my ribcage that's the problem, Mam! Women attract me like magnets, there's nothing I can do about it, I just lose my head.'

Louise Baker bewitched me less than a week ago, as the slates from the prison roof were landing in my garden, hurled by some of the more reckless rioters. Perched on the skylights, they swore to destroy, stone by stone, Her Majesty's ageing correctional facility. The slates mutilated my rosebushes, my peonies and my hydrangeas, my patch of tomatoes and beans, they made the sound the wings of a wounded bird make as

1

they traversed the foliage of my trees before ending their flight among my flowers and vegetables with the dull sound of breaking pottery. A road is all that separates my garden from the southern wall of Strangeways, a wall punctuated by a heavy, wrought iron door surmounted by an old stone pediment. This is the administrative entrance used by judges, police officers, lawyers, prison warders and other personnel. The second entrance, the one used by police vans and visiting families, is a solid, metal, sliding gate in the northern side, that gives on to a narrow, sombre street bordered on one side by the high wall of the prison and on the other by the blackened facades of disused armaments factories, plastered with graffiti and tattered posters. I had placed, on the occasion of this unexpected explosion of violence, a few chairs at the back of my house. Sitting comfortably, on the edge of the garden, one commands a magnificent view over the rebellious prison. One can see the mutineers at the windows, hear their invective, easily read the demands written on the banners they have stretched across from one opening to the next and see more wooden beams being exposed on the roof with each new day. Sometimes smoke from the fires inside the prison is blown over the house, but it is here that one has the best view of the distressing spectacle that, as the hours slip by, is proving disastrous for the preservation of the country's heritage. The mutiny started a week ago. I took in some journalists, for a considerable fee. They were joined later by a few inquisitive members of the public, dressed as though for a night out, who were recommended to me by prison staff, the librarian, the horticulturist and the landlady of the pub where I am a regular. My fee is by no means low, but despite that I cannot meet demand.

Louise holds up her damp, trembling lips to me. Her hips shake vigorously, she thrusts her chest out, her back becomes a magnificent arc in my febrile hands, she murmurs Henry, Henry, Henry, her thighs grip me like a pair of tongs and then suddenly release me as she lets herself go like a blossoming flower. 'When two bodies are united, heaven is never far away,' is another of my mother's sayings. We're approaching heaven, Mam! Oh, Louise, Louise! And what an approach, how tangled, intricate, jumbled up, dissolving, as I melt into the depths of your flesh. Oh, Louise! On this surprisingly mild April evening I turned out almost all the lights before throwing her onto the sofa. Oh, Louise! But music suddenly bursts through the air, music so loud I can no longer hear the blood pulsing in my temples nor the collision of our teeth nor our excited whispers, and then a blinding white light floods the living room and freezes our frolics.

'The Walkyrie,' exclaims Louise, her lovely eyes wide open in wonder, 'the Walkyrie!'

'What?' I cry.

'Can't you hear it? The Walkyrie!'

I feel the floor and the walls trembling, my china rattles in the display cabinet, I see us entwined on an operating table, under a surgical glare without shade, deathly pale, preserved cadavers that have been wheeled out of the morgue. We shall not be going to heaven, Louise! Not this time, no! But Louise doesn't care, she's already getting to her feet, pulling down her skirt to cover her knees once again. She puts on her glasses, buttons up her blouse, straightens her collar and runs to the garden. I see her silhouette on my terrace, her hands on her hips, her nose in the stars, nothing is real any more, we're drowning in the vapour of this white light, this thick light which turns steely blue, blotting out the sky and the night. My eardrums vibrate and the music burrows painfully into the depths of my head. My flowerbeds, my vegetable patch, my hedges, my trees, the garden fence, the wall, the windows, the roofs of Strangeways, all are uniformly bathed in electric sunshine. Batteries of projectors and loudspeakers have been installed on the turrets that have been recaptured from the mutineers: I can make out a helicopter hovering over the prison, a silent hummingbird cutting through the air, noiseless in the din of the music. I see the silhouettes of the gesticulating rioters; perched on chimneys and skylights, they wear balaclavas, they fling slates at the helicopter like furious frisbee players, some brandish sticks and iron bars.

'Do you recognize the Walkyrie now?' Louise shouts in my ear.

'No, I don't!'

'It's Wagner, Henry! Spot on against this background of chaos, don't you think?'

I don't know what to say. I'm surprised the authorities didn't choose Beethoven or Chopin, the only two great composers whose work I know a little. I scream into Louise's ear.

'Why not some swing, like they played after the war, when I was a child?' I see her shrugging and pulling a face as she stares up into the sky. It's true that this is not a post-war atmosphere, we're in the middle of the war here, a siege, with broken glass, slates, bricks, stones, with smashed-up beds, cupboards and windows, with shattered toilet bowls and sinks strewn over the streets and footpaths around the prison. They say that emasculated bodies swing from ropes in the courtyard of the block where the sex offenders were held. The authorities had to register, cross-reference, put on file and then evacuate 1,250 inmates to other prisons within forty-eight hours. These prisoners had given themselves up on the first day of the revolt. There was a parade of police vans escorted by an army of police officers and prison warders in riot gear, and ever since wailing ambulances have been speeding back and forth between Strangeways and Chetham hospital. A screw, John Smith, has already died of a heart attack. He wasn't a bad sort,

4

his obesity made him good-natured; but he was a greedyguts, he used to sneak away from his job and head for the kitchen to dip into the saucepans. For a long time, John was in charge of supervising the distribution of the billycans. He took his cut on an all too regular basis, and became as sizeable as a sumo wrestler within a few years. No longer able to keep up with the trolley bearing the billycans, he had to stop often to catch his breath, which could cause the food distribution to be delayed by up to an hour. This led, one day during the Christmas holidays, to the lags on four floors of one block kicking up such an almighty fuss that the management was forced to ban John from doing that particular job in the prison. Nestling in the soft warmth of his 320 pounds, he was not a man who could endure violence; the emotion must have been too much for a heart enveloped in so many layers of lard.

I place my hands on Louise's generous hips, I stand behind her, I draw her towards me. I breathe in her pert perfume, my lips on her neck, but she frees herself from my embrace, vexed, and takes three steps across the lawn, fascinated by the spectacle, not wanting to miss any of it. I ask her if she is going to write a laudatory article in her rag the following morning – a piece extolling the merits of this son et lumière. She shrugs once again.

'It's the perfect choice of music for the situation, there's no doubt about that, but all the same I think it's a scandal that they decide to flood a residential area with blaring music and light – at one o'clock in the morning – because of what? Because of thirty or forty hotheads occupying a few roofs?'

'It's to stop them sleeping, to wear them out so that they surrender. But I'm fed up with it all! I'm going to be technically unemployed for as long as it takes to repair the damage, and that's all I need with just two years to go before retirement! So let them play Wagner if that's what they want!'

What I said was true. The riot began last Sunday in the

chapel during a service. For once I was not to blame. One of the inmates put a knife to the chaplain's throat, grabbed the microphone and ordered the 300 prisoners in the congregation to overpower the 25 warders present. This took no more than ten minutes and was completed by coshing the screws with socks stuffed with bars of soap and batteries. All they then had to do was take the keys, open up the courtyards and passageways, occupy the central tower and spread the fire of revolt to the eight blocks ranged in star formation around it. The warders had no time to regroup, pull on their riot gear, throw tear gas grenades or charge the rioters, protected by large, transparent shields. They were overwhelmed by groups of mutineers who popped up all over like dandelions in a badly kept lawn. So they abandoned Strangeways to the rebels. We managed to switch off the ovens and put some of the food back in the fridges, but we left without even taking off our aprons, mingling with the warders and the firemen who milled around in disarray. The chapel and Block E were already enveloped in thick smoke which streamed out of the shattered windows; the heat and the flames were tearing the roof apart, slates leapt into the air like caps off bottles of fizzy water. The prison sirens shrieked with all the force of an air raid warning, and the sirens of police cars and vans added to the general racket. Our quiet little area in the north of the city, usually so calm on Sundays, found itself in the middle of a battle. Not a single bird was left in our trees.

The reasons the prisoners gave for their action were not entirely unreasonable. They refused to sleep four or five in a cell made for two, or to stay in their cells twenty-three hours a day; and they demanded more than their current quota of one shower a week. But really, there was no need for them to fall further foul of the law when, if they'd had an ounce of sense, they could have got what they wanted by less confrontational means. A helicopter hovered over Strangeways from dusk till dawn on Sunday night, and early in the morning I saw police, prison and local authority bigwigs talking near the administrative entrance, where they were sheltered from any stones that might be thrown. They were nearly all dressed in navy blue, their official black Bentleys were neatly parked in my street. They had an important air about them, their faces were drawn, sombre, a little lost in this shambles, it seemed to me. As there was no question of going to my work in the kitchens, I went back to bed, preoccupied nevertheless by the gravity of the situation. I sank slowly into an uneasy sleep, I dreamt the kitchens were flooded by at least three feet of greenish, evil-smelling water; the men working at the stoves wore waders, I could hear cries and screams coming from inside the pots and pans. But two hours later, at 9.10 a.m. by my alarm clock, I realized that someone was hammering incessantly at my door. I slipped on my lovely dressing gown – the white one with the black stripes – hurtled down the stairs; vaguely worried, opened the door and found myself confronted by a horde of journalists who machine-gunned me with their flashes before bombarding me with questions. They knew I was the cook at Strangeways. The head cook, I abruptly and nervously corrected them – after all I did have eighteen men under my command. They wanted me to give them details of how the prison was run, what life behind those high walls was like, what sort of food the prisoners were given. I pointed out that it was my duty to be discreet, at which point one of their number vexed me by asking if all my clothes and underwear were cut from cloth that was clearly meant to be worn by prisoners. The chap had the grey skin of a smoker, the emaciated frame of an alcoholic and the long, thin neck of a chicken, with a prominent Adam's apple that rose and fell like a yoyo above the withered bow-tie that dangled over the top of his pink shirt. I was the only one not to laugh. He called me a half-wit under his breath before turning on his heels and marching off, followed by three or four colleagues. But quite a few hacks still clung to my doorstep. The one closest to me, ruddy-faced and sweating, held a ten pound note under my nose and insisted on taking photos of the prison from inside my house. I pocketed fifty pounds that morning – a tenner each from five journalists – and quickly regretted that I had not set a higher entry price. It was a promising catch for them, after all. They hoped to glean from me, in the course of our oh-so-very-cordial conversations, snippets of inside information on the realities of life in Strangeways. And, of course, from my bedroom window and from the attic from where they could gain access to the roof, the view over the south side of the prison, still under the mutineers' control, was simply magnificent. But I gave them not a single newsworthy quote. They took photographs of two prisoners performing a striptease as they perched on a monumental brick chimney, then they left, excited by their haul of images. When television reporters knocked on my door in the early afternoon and asked if they could film day and night from my attic, saying they wanted to install a technician and a reporter, I demanded 150 pounds per twenty-four hours and insisted that they clear off between eleven at night and nine in the morning because I couldn't bear to have strangers overhead when I was sleeping. They didn't bat an eyelid, paid for forty-eight hours up front, and strolled inside with all their gear: video camera, tape recorder, monitor, boom, microphones, radio, and God-knows-what-else, after wiping their feet on my doormat that first rainy Monday in April. I offered them tea. I refused to be interviewed even though I was itching to appear on the ten o'clock news, because I knew too well that the prison hierarchy would not look kindly on such a move. Two stayed to take up their positions by the skylight, where a long transmission antenna had been set up. I forgot about them as the afternoon progressed, a sad afternoon of boredom and technical unemployment – let us not be afraid to call things by their true names. I heard projectiles landing in my garden, causing more damage to the foliage, the flowers and the lawn. Banished from the garden, unable to cook, the only solace left me was Shakespeare, my true companion, who occupies my entire bookcase. I own forty-three editions of the complete works although I've never managed to secure the first edition of 1623. But I wasn't in the mood for reading; I couldn't sit still and so fled my home like a deserter from a besieged castle, to pace around Strangeways to try and gauge the turn of events. My staff identity card enabled me to pass through the cordon of police that ringed the gaol. But it was still near impossible to walk anywhere near the prison walls, even those at the northern and eastern parts, which had been recaptured from the prisoners and from which no more missiles were being flung. The roads there were full of debris that was, in places, embedded in the tarmac like knives in a slab of butter. Bricks, chimney pot pieces and smashed wood blocked the way. I succeeded in getting inside Strangeways by the northern entrance, the one used by police vans and visiting families. At dawn, explosives experts had placed charges at each of the four corners of the heavy metal gate, which was now no more than a crumpled sheet shunted into a corner by a bulldozer. It was through this gaping hole that the squads of prison warders and police made their entrances and exits. A black coach, its windows covered by wire grilles, had been brought in to serve as a command post. I recognized the prison governor, the two chief warders and three other people, one of whom was in uniform, engaged in animated conversation around a table on which plans of the prison were undoubtedly spread. A dozen or so journalists laid siege to the coach, some of them holding their cameras up to the windows to blindly photograph the interior of the vehicle, while a handful of edgy police officers kept them at a distance. I looked up at the two buildings and saw no sign of life at the windows. The vast triangular courtyard was blocked by a double line of mounted police who held their shields and batons in the manner of cavalrymen awaiting the order to charge. From where I stood I could see the horses' rumps, their quivering tails thrashing the air with panache, the riders' black leather-clad backs and white helmets above them – they faced the passageways from which the enemy might at any time pour forth. The electric silence was punctuated by the sharp and irregular clip-clop of hooves on the cobbles, the air was pungent with the smell of tear gas, burnt wood and plastic, to which was added the acrid odour rising from the steaming dung at the horses' feet. I heard the journalists burst out laughing as they read a large banner that sprawled across one of the facades: STEAK FOR DINNER TONIGHT.

An authoritarian voice whispered slowly at my back.

'It's your competence that's at issue here, is it not?'

I turned abruptly, cut to the quick, and began to stammer.

'Good afternoon, Governor, I . . .'

'Your cooking does not appear to be much appreciated, Mr Blain. Still the same old inedible swill.'

'I . . . I'm not in charge of administration, I try to exert some influence, but it's Mr Norton who does the ordering and who chooses the suppliers. I . . . I do what I can to improve things, but . . .'

'It's not a question of improving things for these beggars, Blain, we must make things worse for them! And this has to be done skilfully, so that we are never faced with a riot like this again. Understood, Mr Chief Cook?'

'But Governor, the food wasn't the reason the prisoners gave for the riot, and . . .'

'It may as well have been. Have you read the banner? And what are you doing here anyway? Planning an assault to recapture your ovens? Go on, go home, there's nothing you can do.'

'We're technically unemployed.'

'What do I know about that? I have other fish to fry. We'll be in touch, Blain. Good day.'

The journalists were crowding around us to interview the governor, I pushed through them and went out the way I had come in, cursing the prisoners and horse meat. It was then that I met Louise. I was at a loose end. I found myself in a debris-strewn street wedged between the north wall of the gaol and some disused factories. I decided to go inside one of them, slipping in through a gap in the wall that I had seen before. I sometimes liked to visit these vast spaces, with their cast-iron skeletons and metal gangways cluttered with pulleys, cables and inert, rusting machine tools. For many years prisoners who were trained fitters, metal workers or machine operators would be escorted across the street to work here, in keeping with the tradition that has linked the penitentiary world with the armaments industry since the war. The factory was closed seven or eight years ago, the last squatters evicted earlier this year, and when I'm certain that the place is deserted I like to wander there, reciting lines from *Titus Andronicus*, from *Henry V*, *Henry VI*, or whichever work matches my mood at the time.

> See, ruthless queen, a hapless father's tears:
> This cloth thou dip'dst in blood of my sweet boy
> And I with tears do wash the blood away.
> Keep thou the napkin, and go boast of this

At the moment, for example, it is Richard of York who is embodied in my person – my clear voice rises up, no one can hold back the words in my throat, the echo in the building is as sharp as steel. Sometimes I succumb to childish pleasures here – I gather up old bolts from the ground and fling them at

11

the high windows, which crack under the impact before shattering into a shower of splinters that fall onto the gangways and stairwells. I am happy to be here in the dilapidation of a world that is as old as I am. What's more, I have in recent years had several trysts here, some of which turned sour. Jane, to mention but one, informed me that the darkness of the place matched my soul and my intentions. The old tools, the nails and the screws became weapons, the cables and chains hanging from the roof were like fetters; she claimed she sensed danger, even when our frolics were most fevered, she still looked at me with suspicion, not comprehending the lyricism of this place, that gave our naked bodies a spectacular dimension. One should not impute to people ideas they do not already have, nor should one encourage them to sin, but Jane, effectively, nourished in me unhealthy imaginings.

But this was the first time that I had ever met such a fine creature here by chance. Louise didn't hear me walking through the central workshop, a great nave that once hummed with the sound of workers and machines. I had the uneasy feeling that I was not alone, and started when I heard the click of a camera. I raised my eyes, scanned the labyrinth of metal structures and finally spotted a silhouette on a narrow ledge just under the roof. Cat-like, I silently scaled two storeys in my yellow tennis shoes, which give me the air of a young man. One set of stairs before I reached Louise, I could already contemplate her at my leisure: perched on her high heels, with her slender ankles, her round, firm calves, her stocking laddered just above the back of her left knee, and the generous buttocks that I could make out under the thin, petrol-blue raincoat as she arched her back to lean over a window ledge. She was entirely absorbed in her camera work, she must have had a fine view over the courtyard I had left just minutes earlier; the armoured coach, the blasted gate, the traces of the riot, the banner across the facade, perhaps she could see the mutineers on the roof or in the central tower at which the two buildings converge, she must have been sharp to have found this place from which she could take photos that would be the envy of her fellow reporters when they opened their papers the next morning, this place that would have been of great use to the police to keep watch over events in the prison. To tell the truth, she was actually dressed in a long, pleated, navy blue skirt and wearing large shoes with crepe soles. She was wrapped in a three-quarter length coat, also navy blue; her buttocks, her waist, her figure remained a mystery under these clothes. I would so much have liked her to be not only resourceful, as mother says of women whose company she can tolerate, but also sexy, instead of being like an old governess. I climbed the last flight of stairs, she must have had cloth ears not to have heard me by now. Unsure how best to begin a conversation, I spoke in an offhand manner, like a passer-by addressing a fisherman sitting on the bank of a river.

'Getting some good shots?'

She winced ever so slightly, and replied without turning around.

'Yes, not bad.'

'You're in an isolated, desolate place, a stranger approaches you from behind without warning and you don't bat an eyelid. You're a tough one, I must say.'

'And you, do you like frightening women? Is that it? I heard you coming into the building, I looked down over the guardrail and saw a harmless-looking white-haired man, so I went back to work. One shouldn't always think the worst of people. But perhaps I'm wrong?'

There was mischief in her eyes behind the thick spectacles. She had a peach-coloured complexion, plump cheeks pink from the chilly air, soft, ash-grey, curly hair that reached down over her neck and which she held in place with a slide high up on her head. A few curls fell over her temples, her lips were the

13

colour of strawberries, she was still a beautiful woman who held herself well.

'You're a journalist?'

'Yes, with the *Anglican Tribune*.'

Seeing no recognition in my face, she added:

'It's a paper run by the Church of England in Yorkshire, 20,000 copies sold by subscription, total circulation 60,000, it's in all the newsagents in the region.'

'A parish newspaper, in other words.'

'At the start, yes, fifty years ago, just after the war.'

The view over the part of the prison recaptured from the mutineers was indeed magnificent. One could almost make out the star shape formed by the eight buildings branching out from the central tower, which served as the gaol's surveillance and command centre. I saw the damaged roof, a few small fires still burning, but not a single prisoner on the slates at that time of day.

'You have a fine view from here,' I said. 'But if you want to get some shots of the section of the prison still under the prisoners' control, you should come to my place, on the other side.'

'It's usually herbariums, butterflies, Japanese prints – perhaps you're getting a little carried away by events!'

I've always felt intelligent when I'm on my own, it's only in the presence of women that I feel stupid and threatened.

'True,' I stuttered. 'But I work at Strangeways, I've been chief cook there for twenty years, my house is just across the road, I'm not making this up! The back of my house and the garden look onto the south wall of the prison and the administrative entrance, it's like having the best seats in the theatre, perfect for photos, not so good for my flowers and vegetables, it's like being bombed, it's carnage! There's even a TV crew in my attic, all the pictures you see on ITV are filmed from my house.'

'You can't have many friends if you want my company.'

'I don't want anything, I like your resourcefulness, that's all.'

'All right, then. Let's go. Let me introduce myself: Louise Baker.'

'I'm Henry. Henry Blain.'

She put her two cameras in their cases and we went back down the steep stairs, that made her feel a little dizzy. I told her about the merchant ships I had worked on for many years as a cook, the stairs on those ships are even steeper, almost vertical, and they pitch with the swell. 'That doesn't make me feel any better,' she mumbled. Because of her long skirt, I couldn't see her legs above her knees, despite my favourable position – my head almost directly under her. I could have kissed her ankles, a mere inch away from my lips.

Chapter 11

Last night, after Louise Baker's first visit, I watched the news but saw nothing that had been filmed from my attic. I was furious. I was thinking of Louise, who was probably watching the same programme and not recognizing anything of what she'd been able to observe from my house just three hours before. The news showed mainly aerial shots and images of the northern part of the prison. The prison governor made his speech, confirming that the total surrender of the prisoners was now expected within hours. Dick Bartell, the president of the prison officers' association, declared that this outbreak was a symptom of the very serious problem of the overcrowding in prisons for several years, and that the issue had to be addressed in the House without delay. When the presenter moved on to the next item, the increasing discontent over the poll tax, I leapt from my armchair – despite being nearly sixty years old I'm still nimble in mind and body – and took the two flights of stairs to the attic four at a time. The reporters thought I was bringing them tea – I was a little flushed from my anger, but not out of breath – I was hopping mad. In fact, I shouted at them because they weren't working but were themselves sitting in front of their monitor watching the same news programme. I took a deep breath and asked them straight out whether they were going to film Strangeways from my home or not. I reminded them that they'd been there since the afternoon and had as yet had no apparent effect on the pictures I'd seen on the television. They were embarrassed, stunned at being taken to task like this. The older of the two, the one with a grey moustache and a balding head, tried to pacify me, promising me that they would use their pictures the next day. Seeing that I wasn't convinced, his younger colleague, dressed in leather trousers and a waistcoat whose numerous pockets were stuffed with pens, his brown hair tumbling down over his forehead, three days' beard on his chin, adventurously offered to film my devastated garden with me in the foreground, simply describing – without making any revelations or comments on events inside the prison – the damage caused, as an example of what all local residents whose houses backed on to the prison were suffering, explaining that the mayhem resulting from the mutiny had spread beyond the fortress walls, that the state and the insurance companies must compensate innocent victims.

'Right, then,' I said, suddenly calm, 'let's go.'

But they were reluctant, filming the garden at night would give mediocre results. The scale of the disaster wouldn't come across properly, there would be too much darkness.

'Haven't you got lighting equipment?' I snapped.

They gave in. I made them some tea while they brought their equipment down from the attic. Then I installed myself on the narrow terrace that lies between the house and the lawn, framed by the French windows, with outstretched arm and open hand pointing out the extent of the damage behind me. Their lights illuminated the garden as though it were midday: I could see the foliage of the peonies and the ravaged tomato plants, snapped rhododendron stalks, blossom from the old apple tree lying amidst the broken slates in the furrows of the vegetable patch, stones, bolts, I spotted three whole bricks implanted in the lawn, and to think I had nearly built a conservatory, it would've been pulverized, that's what I said, adding, by way of conclusion:

'The mutineers in Strangeways are under siege, but so are we!'

These words seemed to me sober and discreet and unlikely to vex the prison authorities. The reporters kept saying: 'OK, perfect! Spot on! Perfect, OK!' They were happy with the lighting, and the red glow from the fires on the prison roof created a dramatic atmosphere likely to impress viewers. They retreated to the attic with their gear, they still had two hours up there by the skylight before they could go home for the night. I felt comforted after my little outing in front of the camera, having expressed my distress and spontaneously represented my besieged neighbours, some of whom, even more unfortunate than myself, had had entire sections of slate roof and even window frames flung into their gardens. I settled down on the sofa with a bottle of sherry and must have dozed off at the start of Act II of *Titus Andronicus* because that's where I found my hand at two in the morning, I hadn't heard the reporters leaving the house.

When I woke on Tuesday morning, my first thoughts were for Louise, who, in the freshness of her fifty years aroused in me visions almost pornographic in nature, and that centred around the stairs in the armaments factory, with their smell of rusting metal and oil. I slipped my head under her long pleated skirt, sacrificing the harmony of my hair in the process, and climbed up the inside of her thighs with my lips, occasionally using my tongue to add a little spice to the ascent. But Louise gave no sign of life, I thought for a moment it was her ringing the doorbell – it was nine o'clock in the morning – but it was only the television people returning to their post, telling me conspiratorially that today was a decisive day, that things were going to 'hot up', that they had to be ready to get it all on camera and would have to shoot from both the attic and from ground level, they might even have to run to the end of the garden, climb over my fence and film the lane, the prison walls and the administrative entrance, which was set to be recaptured by the forces of law and order today. I retorted that there was no question of them damaging my wooden fence on top of everything else, they must immediately put the aluminium stepladder in place under the trees.

'OK, OK,' replied the younger one. 'Have you got a helmet you can lend me?'

There was indeed a risk that he would get a brick on the head. I am neither a mason, a miner nor a motorcyclist, but I had the bright idea of offering him my metal colander which I extracted from under the sink – my reporter looked downcast.

'It's better than nothing,' I ventured. 'Besides, you're a strapping lad, you'll be all right!'

He gave me a smile that was more like a grimace. I passed him the stepladder that I kept behind the door, he took it and with his right hand held the colander over his head. He muttered: 'I'm off.' And off he ran, like one of Her Majesty's dutiful soldiers charging into battle in the Falklands war against the degenerate Argentinian usurpers. Within twenty seconds he had disappeared under the cover of my birch trees and the prune tree whose foliage was still meagre in these early days of April, fortunately my big bay trees have evergreen leaves that hid him entirely. We heard him curse – 'My God! What the hell? Shit!' – I shall pass over the choicer profanities, there was the sound of crashing branches and the thump of metal, then he suddenly emerged, running in large zigzags now that he was free of the ladder, I looked at the second hand of my watch, he took the same time, twenty seconds, to cover what was, with all his dodging, probably twice the initial distance. No projectiles landed in the garden, we congratulated him for his courage, a big smile lit up his warrior's face, he returned the colander, I filled a Thermos with piping hot tea and they retreated back up the stairs, the adventure had brought us closer together.

'See you later, Tom! Bye, Jack! Keep your eyes peeled!'

'Yeah, see you later, Henry!'

I think information leaked from the Home Office was circulating among the journalists, they knew the police and the prison officers wanted to storm the prison today, Tuesday. There had been no official denial of rumours that a dozen sex offenders had been tortured, castrated and hanged by their fellow inmates. A young prisoner who gave himself up on the first day of the mutiny told the BBC that the police would find their bodies hanging from the ceilings of the block reserved for sex offenders, those malefactors who were always hated by their fellow inmates. The authorities feared that this barbarous revolt might spread to other jails across the United Kingdom, today would be D-day. That morning I was visited by six more reporters who posted themselves at the back windows of my house, which became a hive of activity filled with the sound of clicking cameras; some of them had three or four strapped across their shoulders and handled them with the dexterity of expert marksmen. I almost pointed out that their pictures would not be terribly original if they were all taking them from the same angle, but I held my tongue and doubled the entry price to twenty pounds per person; earned 120 pounds in two hours, given that my residence, in this road of detached houses, was open to them all day – after all, I was technically unemployed while all my neighbours, manual and office workers alike, left early to go to their jobs and didn't return home until dark.

At exactly 11.23 a.m. – my instinctive reaction was to look at my watch – I heard Jack yelling in the attic. I ran into the garden and saw, at the highest ridge on the prison roof, three inmates unfurling a banner at least twenty yards long on which was written: NO DEAD IN STRANGEWAYS, an attempt, I suppose, to reject the bloood-and-gore news of the neutered and hanged sex offenders. At that moment two armoured vehicles, equipped with water cannons, manoeuvred themselves into the lane. I could see their turrets and cannons swivelling above my bay trees and, coming to a halt, their barrels pointing into the air, before shooting their load. I think all the cameras sprang into action at the same time, as though each reporter had three or four hands to work them. It was the first time I had seen water cannons in action, smooth, solid rods of water gushed out of them like granite and only began to crumble a few yards from the funambulist prisoners, who had skedaddled off to hide behind a chimney stack. They looked like they were having a good time; they stripped off for us and mimicked honest citizens taking a shower in their bathrooms, they scrubbed their backs, they washed under their arms, they soaped their crotches, the noise of the pumps and the surging water filled the air with a deafening racket. When the tanks were empty, the two vehicles turned around and headed back towards the administrative entrance under a volley of missiles that suddenly began to rain down on them as though the clouds were dropping stones on the earth. The bombardment was all the more exciting for the fact that the perpetrators remained invisible behind the walls, which made their aim approximate and resulted in yet more debris arriving in my garden. Calm was suddenly restored. In great frustration, I grabbed a plastic bag, attached the colander to my head with the help of a long elastic band that I passed through the two handles and under my chin, and began gathering up the junk strewn across my garden. I could no longer bear my forced inactivity, Louise was still playing dead, I had to do something to make the time pass. But after about an hour, by which time I had filled two large rubbish bags with the most diverse detritus – stones, lead piping, a flask of surgical spirit, vices, a reel of copper wire, an electric counter, a spanner – a brick and a piece of cast-iron radiator came flying through the air and embedded themselves in the grass not more than a yard from my feet. I jumped with fright and beat a hasty retreat, cursing this mess that looked like it was never going to end. I wolfed down two fried eggs and a slice of bacon – the photographers were gone, I told Tom and Jack that I'd be out for the whole afternoon – and went walking. In fact, I was thinking I would go and see my horticulturist and buy a tarpaulin with which to cover the garden. I took the bus to Oaklands and then walked for a good five minutes through this suburb that merges into the countryside to the north of Manchester.

Turning off Sherbrook Avenue, with its gleaming houses, the little street on the right, where Romeo has his garden centre, seems to have been entirely forgotten by the roadworks department. There are potholes in the road and the pavements are in a terrible state. But my mind is on other things, all my thoughts are on Louise and on the sense of menace that I feel growing ever stronger inside me, I don't look where I'm putting my feet, twice my right shoe plunges into puddles of muddy water, shit! shit! shit! I'm raging by the time I get to the shop, I grunt a vague greeting and ask Elizabeth for a sponge and a basin of water to clean my shoes and my trouser legs. I whisper 'Thank you, Juliet', which always makes her blush. She replies as she usually does:

'You know how it ends, don't you? You want to see us all buried!'

Today, I respond in a murmur, 'Don't put ideas in my head.'

But she doesn't hear me.

The shop is huge. Birds and multi-coloured budgies chirp in three cages hanging from the ceiling, a few hamsters give little high-pitched cries as they run inside wooden wheels that make bells tinkle as they turn. The shop smells of damp humidity, the flowers, the soil and the seeds, the odour so strong that you might think you've walked into an oil mill. I moisten, I rub, I rinse, that's it, clean, I become a nice person again.

'Is Romeo here?'

'Yes. You know the way.'

I thread my way to the dark backroom, the walls of which are covered in shelves and drawers, I meet the deaf and dumb brother-in-law who, in his grey overall, seated on an old office chair, his chest almost parallel with the desk, does the books, manages the stock and places the orders. Sensing a presence in the room he lifts his head just a fraction, looks over the top of his glasses, creases his nose and his brow, raises his upper lip, which gives his countenance an oddly twisted look, and emits a nasal grunt before finally recognizing me; his face now lights up with a smile that reaches almost to his ears. 'Hello, Charles,' I say, not knowing what to say, and head for the door at the back that leads to the 2,000-square-yard garden where the plants are stocked in containers on the ground. I walk down one of the paths that are straight as a die and wide enough to let Romeo, draped in his blue smock, standing proud as a peacock, be driven around in a trailer pulled by the miniature tractor. Ten yards away I see his two workers, red-headed twins from Scotland who have obeyed him slavishly for the last twelve years. They mature the soil, pot and de-pot plants, plant and pull up, take delivery of stock, wrap and unwrap, but at the moment they're handling compost and I don't stop. They tell me that Romeo is in the azalea and rhododendron greenhouse, which is at the other end of the plot. I note that Romeo still writes, with his ample and flowing hand, the names of the plants on the pretty plastic grey and black labels; the ashes that he has always spread over the paths crunch under my soles. I go through the glass arch, assailed by the warm, humid air, I catch sight of his snow-white hair through the thick and glistening foliage of a tall camellia.

'The peat isn't enough on its own. You need to add dried blood. Hello, Henry. You don't look happy, is your mother at you again?'

Romeo still has a slight Italian accent, a Mantua accent, as he frequently points out. He met Elizabeth thirty years ago on a beach in Cornwall while he was attending a horticultural conference in Bath, he was seduced by her fine features, her pallid complexion and her calming silence, and was captivated by the luxuriance of the English countryside, by English gardens, and by the infinite range of greenery to be found here.

'Have you got any tarpaulins?' I ask him. 'To cover the garden.'

'What? A 500-square-yard tarpaulin? To cover the garden? You planning to put up a circus tent? Can I be your juggler and accordion player?'

'It's not funny, Romeo. I'm bombarded day and night, I have to do something!'

Romeo doesn't understand. I ask him if he ever watches the news on television, he jibs, he gets annoyed.

'Do you take me for an imbecile? I watch the news twice a day, I know full well that that crook Thatcher is trying to screw us with her poll tax! I see her sending in her mounted police against demonstrators, and . . .'

'I wasn't talking about that. I meant the riot at . . .'

'Strangeways, of course I know about it, I was talking to Elizabeth about it just yesterday, I was saying if it went on like that poor Henry will be laid off until it's over!'

I ignore this comment, I remain calm, I take up my sentence at the point where Romeo interrupted me, I explain the situation, he punctuates my tale with: Holy God! Holy Mother of God! Jesus! Mary Magdalen! Saint Peter of the Vatican! Christ! God Above! etc.

'But I don't have a tarpaulin that size! They don't make

them. And even if they did you wouldn't be able to put it in place. It'd be too heavy, you'd need to have it a yard above the ground, and then there're the trees to think about. Besides, everything would turn yellow without the light, it's mid-April. No, what you need are nets to protect the flower beds and the seedlings. They're fifty square yards each, they're light and easy to handle, and you can hook them up no problem.'

We leave the greenhouse, he leads me to a large, corrugated iron shed where his tools and his red tractor are stored. He shows me the nets, which are made of plastic.

'The problem is that there are only two of them. I'd have to order you eight more. But it'd take a week for them to arrive and by then the riot would be over. If you'd come to me straight away on Monday morning, I'd have ordered them then and they'd have been here by tomorrow lunchtime. Why don't you buy yourself protective clothing, you know, like American football players, then you could run out and pick up the stones, you could even ward them off as they rain down on the garden. You'd be a young man again!'

'It's not funny, Romeo, I'm not laughing, and . . .'

'It'll all be over in two days! Don't worry, we'll be able to sort out your garden.'

I take the bus back the way I came. A dirty drizzle drips down on the town, the afternoon is drawing to a close. I'm put out, Romeo didn't realize the seriousness of the situation, it probably suited him not to. But Louise had been sympathetic when she came by yesterday, she had used half a roll of film photographing the garden when she saw what a mess it was in. I miss my stop. I'm so preoccupied. Until a couple of days ago I was peacefully preparing for my retirement; I would spend my weekends with my mother in Liverpool, I would fish from Prince's Dock, daydreaming by the estuary, calmly savouring my old age, but now here I am assailed from all sides. I get off at the next stop, in Oak Street, and call in to see Suzan, who runs a pub there like a queen rules over a kingdom. The words Suzan Carlos Simson are written on the shiny wooden facade, and further along is the word Pub. An earthenware pint glass hanging from a wrought iron gallows creaks in the wind above the door. Six customers at the bar, a dozen seated at tables – the two bar staff who assist Suzan begin work at six o'clock – the place still smells of bleach, damp floorcloths and stale smoke. I order a pint of Guinness at the bar, Suzan winks at me.

'See those lovers over there in the corner, Henry? I'm making them some sandwiches, they're hungry, the poor things; and after I'll come and have a chat with you.'

'When you say that I feel like an old man at death's door.'

'You're either in a foul mood or you've got something on your mind. I'll be right back.'

I head for a table, flick through *The Sun*, on the front page they're predicting that the mutineers are about to surrender. 1,560 detainees have already been shunted off to other prisons, there are only eighty mutineers left holding a few buildings. Here's Suzan coming to sit next to me with another pint of Guinness destined for my lips. She really is a fine specimen, with her peasant's build, her broad hips, generous breasts, solid shoulders, nimble fingers, her witch's nails painted emerald green – the colour of her eyes – her freckled face, her curly red hair tumbling down over her shoulders in waves.

'Like all redheads, Suzan, you bring bad luck. You'd never catch me caressing your pretty bum.'

'You old lech! I'll give you a box on the ear in a minute, that'll calm you down.'

Suzan has an easy charm which envelopes her clients in its carnal, perfumed intimacy, each and every one of her regulars believes that he and she form an exclusive pair of old accomplices, such is the magnetic force she exudes.

'Stop messing around and tell me what's happening at the prison.'

'It's like what it says in the papers except more dramatic because the locals, me included, are having a particularly hard time of it. God knows why they ever built houses so close to such a place!'

'True, life would definitely be less turbulent if you lived next to a cemetery.'

'Why are you saying that?'

'Calm down! Don't you remember I lived by the entrance to Fenwick cemetery for four years? You know in the suburbs you can end up just as easily beside a prison, a cemetery or a run-down hospital.'

'The only things that are ending up anywhere at the moment are slates, and they're ending up in my garden.'

And I tell her just as I told Romeo about the state of the garden and the neighbours' roofs, except this time, telling the story yet again, I sink deep into despair.

'So you're not doing any cooking these days. Maybe you could come and give me a hand, you could do the roast beef and mixed veg. But you'd need to look after my customers a bit better than you did your prisoners!'

The invitation is tempting. If Louise doesn't come back and I end up sitting all day in my bunker.

'It's really nice of you to offer, Suzan, really nice, but I can only say maybe at the moment, I'll have to talk to Louise about it, maybe, why not.'

'You've got a Louise in your life and you haven't told me about it!'

'Well, I'm not quite there yet, we're working on it.'

'And you're still miserable as sin! It must be very hard work.'

'Do you know the *Anglican Tribune*? 20,000 subscribers, circulation 60,000.'

'No, why? Are you . . .'

'No reason. I'll let you know next week. OK?'

'Whenever you want, Henry Blain. You know that we've always got room for you here.'

I leave Suzan's place comforted. The night has come, it sparkles with neon and street lights, I stride happily along the asphalt road. Suzan's proposition has given me the perspective I needed to put some order back in my existence. I let my eye wander over the glittering shop windows until I arrive at the entrance to my estate, which is normally deserted. Since Sunday though, its streets have been getting busier every day. People from the area come to watch the show after their day's work; or rather they come to drink in the siege atmosphere – they can't get beyond the line of police that blocks their path seventy yards from the prison. Only the roads running perpendicular to the prison offer any sort of view, but that is a poor one of the walls, and nothing can be seen of the mutiny apart from the occasional explosions of teargas canisters or Molotov cocktails. All the fires seem to have been brought under control.

I quicken my step, I notice a man has set up a stall selling chocolate and candy floss on the corner of my street and the one that leads to the administrative entrance – he must be tickling the police officers' noses with his smells of sugar and chocolate. I open my letterbox and find only junk mail – Louise hasn't left a message – I dread the empty sadness of the night that lies before me. I take a bottle of sherry and three glasses up to the attic. Tom and Jack look bored. They're sitting on stools, their elbows resting on their knees, they've switched their monitor to BBC1, which is showing a report on Iraq. We watch Saddam Hussein and his family posing in their living quarters in exotic casual wear. Everyone is smiling, it's cool there in the shade, we hear the burble of a fountain in the flower-filled interior garden. The mosaics are beautiful, they cover the floors and the walls; the decor is beautiful, the people are beautiful. I'd like to know the sweet pleasures of that life, I'm sick of the one I have, this life devoid of miracles.

'Why are you watching the competition?' I ask in surprise.

'There's only game shows on ITV at the moment. We're waiting for the nine.'

'The nine?'

'The nine o'clock news. It's been another wasted day here. We thought they were going to storm the prison, but all they did was blast them three times with the water cannon and then leave again. If we can sell two minutes of that we'll be doing well. What the hell are the police up to? The Home Office bigwigs promise us the Guns of Navarone, and then – nothing!'

'And when I think that this morning I risked life and limb to put that ladder up at the end of the garden,' remarked Jack.

'Yeah, particularly since I'll be needing it tomorrow to do some work on the house!'

Jack turns pale. I serve both of them a generous measure of sherry.

'Here,' I say, 'this will help boost morale. Are you coming back tomorrow?'

'The haven't told us yet. But probably.'

'Because the money your station paid me was for forty-eight hours and tomorrow the meter starts running again. You'd better tell your boss. I know, I know, but that's not the point, Tom. You're both really nice guys but business is business. Right then, let's have another little drink. Cheers.'

It upsets me to see them so frustrated by the situation. I leave them in the company of Saddam's wife and children, I go downstairs to prepare my dinner, cold chicken with potatoes, cabbage, and celery with walnuts and yoghurt. Then I sit on the sofa with my tray, in front of the television, which I switch to ITV – I watch the game shows and wait for the news.

Luckily, I have twenty-five minutes to swallow my meal before the opening titles roll, announcing the day's catastrophe in Cinemascope. The Strangeways mutiny is no longer the top story. I have to put up with the poll tax, the inflation rate at 8 per cent, confirmation that unemployment has gone down for the second consecutive month, before they get to the prison mutiny. They say that a hundred prisoners are still holding four buildings in the south and east wings, the pictures are filmed from helicopters – there are gaping holes burnt in to the roof. Then come the shots taken from my house. The newsreader emphasizes that the mutineers have denied rumours reported by the BBC that thirteen people have been hanged inside the gaol. I see what I saw this morning from my place: the three prisoners unfurling their banner: NO DEAD IN STRANGEWAYS, and having their shower on a chimney stack. The newsreader struggles to remain serious, he notes that the predicted surrender has not come, then in a more sombre tone he speaks of the forgotten victims of the riot: the local people whose gardens and roofs have been damaged by missiles thrown from the gaol. It's me! This time it's me on the screen; it's dark, the electric light creates too much contrast, the contours of my cheeks and my chin are bluish black, with my three-day beard and the bags under my eyes I look like a refugee, I look as if my body is aching. I'm standing there, very stiff and trembling, I make a theatrical gesture towards the garden, the scale of the disaster spreads out like the end of the world at the end of my outstretched arm. I like myself, I am a respectable victim deserving of compassion, I admire myself unreservedly, if only there wasn't that lighting from below that makes me look like Dracula, with orangy pink blotches on my cheekbones and forehead. My voice is warm, vibrant, too human perhaps, when I say: 'The prisoners in Strangeways are under siege, but so are we, the poor people who live next to the prison!' Then the newsreader speaks again to ask who will compensate the inhabitants of this modest neighbourhood. The end. Now he's discussing the commercial tensions between Japan and the United States. I turn off the sound, knock back my glass of beer in one go, climb back up the stairs, Tom and Jack greet me with collusive smiles, I want to kiss them but contain myself. I speak loudly.

'Bravo, boys! Lovely report, truthful, moving, even if you did improvise it. When you know how . . .'

'It's you who should be congratulated, Henry, you come across really well on TV, you know?'

They tell me that nothing important will happen tonight, they had a call from head office on their mobile, they can go home. I see them to the door, they turn down my offer of one for the road, I don't have time to say goodbye – the telephone rings. I rush to the dining room and knock over the tray, there are potatoes all over my carpet, yoghurt seeps into the wool. I fulminate, but maybe it's Louise wanting to talk to me about my interview.

'Hello?'

I hear a dull hubbub punctuated by the clink of glasses and distant bawling.

'Hello?'

'Henry? It's Suzan. Can you hear me? I can barely hear you with this racket. You were really good on the telly, you know? Very convincing! A bit like a Red Indian, but it's all about technique. A few of the regulars recognized their old mate Henry, if you decide to come and work in the kitchen here you'll get a standing ovation.'

'Oh, Suzan, you're too nice to me. I really appreciate it, I almost want to say yes straight away.'

'Take your time. I just wanted to tell you that after we saw you on the box we all felt for you. I just had to phone you. Listen, Henry, some of the customers asked me if they could come over to your place, just to have a look. You're on the front line, so to speak, as Willie was saying just now.'

'Well, er, to tell the truth, I'm charging admission, Suzan. Not for you, of course, but for the journalists and any strangers who turn up. It's half-price, ten quid, for the non-professionals. I think that's fair, they're not gaining anything from it. It's a job, you know. My address is made public, I get . . .'

'You don't miss a trick! Just don't let it all go to your head, darling. But I suppose you're right to take advantage of the situation. Anyway, I'll pass the information on, and maybe I'll come along as your guest one day. Bye, love.'

I like Suzan. The reticence I heard in her voice bothers me but nevertheless I'm not going to turn down the badly needed cash my activities are bringing in. If the Commons or the Home Office doesn't declare the place a disaster area, the insurance companies won't pay out a penny for the damage. But I was happy about the impact of my media performance – I'll be bought quite a few drinks the next time I go to Suzan's. The phone rings once again and I answer it immediately.

'Hello?'

'Henry? Holy Mother of Christ! What an ordeal! Listen, I'm really sorry about not taking you seriously this afternoon. It was only when I saw the state of your garden that I realized how bad things really were. Jesus, Mary and Joseph! Elizabeth had to calm me down, didn't you, Eliza? I was quite shaken, wasn't I, Eliza? So much hatred and violence! There are of course some folk who are unjustly imprisoned, but, mercy me, I really was appalled by those brigands. Oh, Henry!'

'I'm touched, Romeo!'

'Don't worry, as soon as this nightmare is over I'll help you restore your Arcadia, you can count on me. I was thinking of coming over to assess the damage, I'll bring Charles and Elizabeth with me and we can all have a coffee together. I was thinking: your house has become like a box in a theatre, from where you can see all the action, the tragedy that's taking place before your very eyes. In spite of everything you're the guest of honour, you're a fine example, you know, of the innocent spectator plunged into History!'

Romeo is not a mere garden-centre owner, he's a gardener in the most noble sense of the term. He's an educated man who has been able to blend England and Italy in his life. When we discuss gardens created in the French style, the Italian, the English or the Japanese, I feel cultivated, erudite, sensitive! I see colours, leaves, branches, I understand the scale of things, I see space! One day I shall speak with him of Shakespeare, one day when we are true friends, for I am simply one of his oldest customers at the moment. This is the first time that he has deigned to offer to come to my home, he knows my garden thanks to the photographs and the plans I've shown him, I'd always feared that he would never come to look at my work. Life is unjust. Today he agrees to visit me and all he will see is a devastated piece of earth. I finish my sherry, sponge the yoghurt from the carpet and pick up the potatoes that have rolled under the sofa. I want to tidy up my living-cum-dining-room-cum-study. I'm certainly not unhappy with the inter-view; the neighbours will be grateful that I've become the spokesman for our cause, maybe we could form an association for the defence of people living near Strangeways. My job at the prison would probably prevent me from becoming president but I don't care, I'm not ambitious, I've always preferred the shade of the kitchen. But I can't clean the room up at my leisure. The phone keeps ringing, it's some prison warders I'm friendly with, an assistant cook, an old friend I haven't heard from in a year, congratulations rain down on me, as do requests to come to my place to have a look, to bring the family, the neighbours. I state my price, anyone who won't cough up stays at home! Every time I pick up the receiver I have the wild hope that it'll be Louise and my disappointment grows. I become indifferent to the compliments, the praise and the warm expressions of solidarity. At eleven o'clock, I've done nothing with my evening. I return from the kitchen with a damp sponge when the telephone rings again – this is the last time I'm going to answer it.

'Hello?'

'It's me, Henry, I've been trying to get through all evening, what the hell are you up to? You'd think it was the Blitz to hear you, son, the V1s and the V2s and all that business, and why not meteorites while you're at it! Mars attacks Earth! A bit of self respect, Henry! You're your mother's son, your mother who was decorated, lest you've forgotten. I saw you with your lovely white hair and your fancy make-up posing like a soldier returning from the front and I burst out laughing! I'll have to pretend I'm sick tomorrow to get out of lunch at the widows' club. What am I going to tell them? I was so happy, I shouted: "That's my Henry on the telly!" and then it all turned sour. I can't stay on any longer, sorry, I'm phoning from the Hartleys', we'll talk during this week. Bye, Henry.'

It's cold – I have to turn the thermostat up – I'm shivering, it starts in the small of my back and radiates up to my shoulders. My head is sore, I think I can feel a bad cold coming on. I pop two aspirins and put the kettle on to make myself a cup of piping hot tea. I have a last glass of sherry while I wait for it to boil. At eighty-seven, mother has lost none of her authority, an authority that draws its strength from her own heroic past as well as that of her husband; from the loss of a son, my elder brother, a young Spitfire pilot in the RAF – returning from a mission, he went down over the Channel. Mother has condensed within herself, like an essential oil, all authority in the family. She sees matters as they are, she's a good judge of things – I'm too caught up in my gardening problems – she's right, I must've been exaggerating, I went a bit overboard on the telly, my taste for the theatrical, the great Shakespearean tragedies and historical dramas have clouded my mind. I can't stop shivering, my shoulders tremble uncontrollably, my teeth chatter, I'll have to call her back: 'Mother, I'm really sorry I upset you, that I messed up your lunch at the club, I thought ... I thought ... well, I wasn't really thinking at all, dear mother, I'm so sorry, but I don't have the Hartleys' number. I wipe the crumbs from the coffee table, I try to get rid of the yoghurt stain on the carpet, the kettle's boiling, I make the tea, I take a deep breath, tears come to my eyes, fever taking hold of me no doubt. I sit down on the sofa, I pour the tea, I calm myself, Henry, calm down, old friend, Henry, old mate, calm down! Time for bed, tomorrow is another day. Life goes on.

Chapter III

I'd stopped expecting Louise by the time she arrived on Thursday afternoon. She'd abandoned her governess's outfit and was wearing a pair of flat-soled moccasins, a red and green pleated skirt that stopped at her knees, a white blouse with an alluring lace collar, and a light, navy blue jacket. The sun was shining, and she seemed like a nymph appearing to announce the arrival of spring. Her ash blond hair was tied in a perfect bun. I would happily have advised her to get herself a set of contact lenses, to get rid of those goggles on the end of her nose. She says hello, we don't really know what to say to each other, she shows me yesterday's *Anglican Tribune*. I recognize my garden, which she photographed on Monday, and above it the worrying headline: 'Rioters ransack Strangeways area', which sounds like the prisoners are getting out of the gaol and carrying out raids on the town. She's also brought the paper from two days ago. I recognize two photographs taken from the old armaments factory, accompanied by a more reassuring caption: 'On the second day of mutiny, the police recaptured several buildings'. I invite her in for a glass of brandy. She refuses, I insist, we can't stand out here on the step all day. With a nod I gesture towards the journalists and rubbernecks dawdling on the footpath – particularly in front of my house –

for whom we're becoming a spectacle. She agrees to come in for ten minutes, no more, she just wanted to tell me that her paper hadn't forgotten me, it was interested in ordinary people's problems. I had to some extent cut the ground from under her feet by giving that interview to the television people.

'But it's not the same thing at all, Louise! I mean, Miss Baker. Do you mind if I call you Louise? Thank you. Television, Louise, is ... it's something that's aimed at everybody. But what really touches me is that someone like you could be sufficiently interested in my case to write something about me in black and white, a text that ... that's ... it's as if it's addressed to me alone, like a letter!'

I smile brightly at her, I'm pleased with my reply. Louise's cheeks turn a light red, she looks like she might be an emancipated spinster, she knows what she wants, she's in charge, but she's not impervious to a man's compliments. She walks ahead of me in the corridor. I admire her figure, the way she carries her head, her broad shoulders, the arch of her back, the roundness of her buttocks, the fullness of her calves, ah, Louise, my hands are itching to take hold of you, how I want to lay you on the kitchen table, hitch your skirt up, rumple your blouse, sniff your neck, humming *God Save The Queen* between our burning kisses. Ah, Louise, who stops short in the kitchen after looking through the door into the dining room.

'I didn't realize you had guests,' she murmurs.

I hope that is a note of disappointment I hear in her voice at the fact that we are not alone. At the moment there are seven people sitting on chairs arranged in a row on the narrow concrete terrace, which I've laid with lovely rustic tiles. They have their backs to us, four men and three women, four bare heads, a woman wearing a hat with a veil, a bowler hat, and a checked cap. They're very well behaved, some of them whisper in their neighbour's ear, their eyes are fixed on the walls and roofs of Strangeways, all is calm, there's absolutely nothing going on, they stare at a wall that was built in 1860 or therabouts. Those with the right to a chair are the Recommended or Anonymous Rubbernecks, the RARs; the others, the Professional Reporters at Work, the PRWs, wander from the end of the garden to the attic and back again, the cellar is the only place out of bounds – they may use all the windows that give onto the prison, they make the best use they can of their time because they're in a hurry and they never stay longer than half an hour. For the RARs, however, who may well stay for the whole day, I issue tickets with a time written on them – they're allowed to stay for two hours of the show. I unearthed some old writing pads and used white paper for the RARs, blue for the PRWs. Everyone returns their receipt as they leave, I don't want any trace of my business escaping into the outside world. As I explain my doings to Louise I think I can see a growing sense of astonishment and even admiration in her eyes, eyes that are much enlarged by her thick lenses.

I began organizing myself yesterday morning, the day after my television interview, because demand for my services had grown rapidly: ten reporters and seven rubbernecks turned up on Wednesday alone, four of them sent my way by Eddy, an assistant cook, and by a screw I was vaguely friendly with, a chap who grumbles rather than speaks, who has worms and who's happy to scratch the cleft between his buttocks in front of anybody and everybody. Two others were blokes I knew from Suzan's place. I haven't included Tom and Jack among the ten reporters – they arrived yesterday morning with their producer and I gave them a 25% discount on the initial tariff, in return for which they paid up front until Sunday, regardless of the course events take. Having learnt from Wednesday's experience, I decided to start issuing tickets and to invent a vague set of rules about the length of time people could stay. To the four seats from the dining room I added three folding chairs that I use in the summer when I want to dine al fresco.

What's more, the fifty-odd mutineers provided us with a good show yesterday. They appeared at the windows overlooking our gardens, they made friendly gestures at us, gesture which I for my part refused to reciprocate, they stretched from one window to another a long banner proclaiming: NO SURRENDER, and then at the end of the morning ten of them clambered up onto the roof, carrying voluminous bin liners on their backs and another banner as big as the one that two days ago had declared: NO DEAD IN STRANGEWAYS. It took them a good twenty minutes to fasten the thing onto the wooden beams. It was then that I realized that they too had seen me on the television, for they were now asking the locals to forgive them for the damage they'd caused. It was written there on black and white on their banner: SORRY, DEAR NEIGHBOURS, FOR THE TROUBLE. SORRY! Then they undid the strings that tied the rubbish bags, plunged their arms in up to their armpits and, like magicians, began to throw up into the air hundreds and hundreds of the paper flowers they make in their workshops. Roses, narcissi, dahlias, lilies, daisies. Jack hurtled down two sets of stairs, the camera pressed to his chest; like a zealous centre-forward on a rugby team, he didn't even look at me even though I was trying to hand him the colander: for his head. He pushed past the spectators who blocked his access to the garden and ran straight for the cover of my trees. I heard him cursing again: Blast! Blast! Shit! Shit! The sound of rustling leaves gave me cause to worry about my young plants, I realized he was desperately searching for the bloody ladder which he had risked his life to place there the day before. I had of course told him I'd be needing it to do a spot of work in the kitchen, but as I'm not a bad sort I ran out to him with the ladder under my arm. I didn't even get out of breath, that must mean I'm in pretty good shape for my close to sixty years. Louise will be opening her arms and thighs for a man who is still in shape! Jack was crimson with irritation, I tiptoed away, he was still ranting: Hell! Hell! Shit! Blast! Then I saw his head emerge above the bay trees, camera on his shoulder, and under the April sky he filmed the flowers fluttering down onto the tarmac and the rubble, brightening the devastated street with a multitude of colours. It was such an unexpected event that my spectators burst into applause so vigorous it nearly brought the house down. Jack was scream- ing with joy, his eye glued to the viewfinder, capturing the images with a series of low-angle shots. It was when these pictures were broadcast, not only on ITV but also on both BBC1 and BBC2, that the Strangeways uprising started to become popular. That evening, snatches of my interview were shown again to enable viewers who had missed the previous episode to understand the reason for the message on the banner and for the thousands of flowers with which the prisoners showered the neighbourhood. Needless to say, my phone started ringing non-stop after that, and this morning, from 9.30 onwards, I've had, as they say, a full house, there are seven bums on my seven seats. There are two viewing sessions in the morning.

Louise stands dumbfounded in the dining room doorway, I want to tell her all about my big day, Wednesday 4 April, but she interrupts me immediately, there's no need, she saw it all on the television, she was even moved by it, it fleshes out my personality a little more to know that I was able to mollify the mutineers. It also shows, she preaches confidently, that men whose souls are supposedly lost are still capable of feelings for others, human nature remains unfathomable; the article she wrote pleading my case and that of my neighbours would be more balanced were she to write it today. I say nothing, I listen, I look, I pour her a glass of brandy and offer her some biscuits, we sit on my Formica chairs. The only thing she ever drinks is port after a meal, to go with crackers and cheese, but today, as an exception, she will clink glasses with the 'hero of the day', 'of yesterday and the day before', I correct her. She smiles and takes a sip, the alcohol immediately makes her immense green eyes glisten. I'm happy, Louise has returned.

'Come on, let's have another one! Cheers!'

Alcohol quickly dissolves the barriers between people and on the second glass Louise loosens up and blossoms like a parched flower that has just been watered. The ten minutes she'd granted me have long passed. She talks about herself, tells me she's a campaigner for the Church of England in Lancashire: for more than twelve years she's run a choir in the disadvantaged area of Rochdale, in the east of the city, yes, she trained as a pianist before turning to journalism, she liked reporting, going to the scene of events, she always chose stories about poverty or social injustice, once she'd even exposed a financial scandal in which old folk placed in a particular hospice ended up losing all their savings. The management of the establishment had tricked them into signing over power of attorney, and the extorted funds were channelled through several willing helpers in a selection of banks. The national press got wind of the affair and Louise was promoted to chief reporter. Now she can write whatever she likes on whichever subject she likes: sport, art, society, justice, she has carte blanche. I congratulate her and in her honour we raise our glasses, filled for the third time with brandy. Now it is not only her eyes that are shining, her cheeks and her ears are glowing. Ah, Louise, your entire face is ablaze. But suddenly, two of my spectators appear in the kitchen, the man in the bowler hat, followed closely by the woman with a perm – white curls sprinkled with purplish highlights.

'Excuse me, but we've been here nearly an hour and nothing has happened. What are we supposed to do?'

'How should I know? Try admiring the architecture, the sky, the shape of the clouds, the paper flowers...'

'I was told you worked in the prison and...'

'I do, but that doesn't mean I can make the prisoners perform at will.'

'Then you'll have to reimburse us. You're selling tickets as if this were a theatre, but the stage is empty.'

'Do you really expect me to be able to guarantee the march of History?'

'Well, you should've warned us before you took our money!'

I don't dare insult them in the presence of Louise, him with his bank manager's deportment and her, an old whore constantly nodding her head like a plucked chicken; if it wasn't for Louise I'd give them a good kick in the posterior and chuck them straight out. But I say no more, return their now crumpled ten pound notes, take back my tickets. They leave with the air of an indignant lord and lady. Louise can barely stop herself laughing, I drain my glass, as though to change the subject she asks me if it's dangerous to go into the garden to have a look at the paper flowers. Louise totters, she takes my arm to steady herself, her hand is soft and light. I lead her to the bay trees, apologizing on the way to the remaining five spectators, who are chattering happily, for disturbing them. We dive into the bushes, the stepladder is still there, I help Louise climb up it. She staggers at every step, she giggles, she gives piercing little shrieks. I think of the stairs in the armaments factory, I follow the curve of her legs, stop at the seam of her stockings, contemplate the band of soft white flesh at the top of her thighs, then fix my eyes on her little lace panties, which, to my great surprise, are red, while her suspenders, also made of lace, are navy blue – the Union Jack, I think. But thoughts of the national colours are fading already, this intimate view of Louise is beginning to hurt my eyes. I experience a truly gustatory excitement, my gastric juices are flowing, I . . .

'It's so beautiful!' interrupts Louise, looking at the pot-holed, debris-strewn road. 'Flowers, growing from the ruins of a prison! It's life and hope reasserting themselves, isn't it, Henry?'

I let her gawp, her head above the evergreen foliage. I concentrate on the unruly strands of pubic hair that peep out past the elastic of her knickers. Ah, Louise! My mouth will soon be exploring the dark secrets of your thighs!

'What was that, Henry?'

'Your excitement is touching. You, you . . . you have the soul of a poet, Louise, I . . .'

'Stop making fun of me, Henry!'

I hear the doorbell, I beg Louise to hold on tightly to the ladder. I run through the garden and the house and throw open the door; it's Romeo, Elizabeth and Charles dressed up as though they were off to the opera. I'm disconcerted, I step aside, they march in as though entering a dying man's house, Romeo embraces me, in the Italian fashion, he says. His wife tells him to show some respect, Charles smiles exaggeratedly, he gestures and makes faces at me. He's expressing, I believe, his satisfaction at being here, he blows his nose, I look at my shoes. I lead them into the kitchen, I want to give them a drink, but Romeo whispers that they're in a hurry, they want to see the garden and the prison straight away. They seem entirely unsurprised by the wandering journalists and the seated spectators.

'It's not dangerous, is it, Henry? When we saw the prisoners on the telly paying homage to the locals I said to Elizabeth: they've signed a truce, now is the time to head for Henry's!'

He greets the assembly as though he's about to make a speech, the ruffle on his white shirt quivering like a white muslin sheet hanging out to dry in the machine room of an old cargo boat. As he strides into the garden, Louise, still slightly unsteady, advances towards us. I do the introductions, but when I say: 'Romeo, a great gardener,' Louise adds: 'By appointment to Her Majesty The Queen?', then guffaws and breaks into hiccoughs. Everyone's shocked, except Charles, whose face remains impassive. The company of a tipsy Louise was very congenial a moment ago, but now that my distinguished guests are here I have the almost uncontrollable urge to slap her in the face, a good whack that would leave the violet mark of my hand on her white cheek, that'd make her snap out of it, make her pull herself together! Elizabeth and Romeo turn away, only Charles is still facing her. A huge grin spreads over his face, his lovely horsey teeth sparkle, his upper body is shaken with spasms, which makes Louise laugh manically. I leave them to it and join Romeo, who has moved a few yards away.

'My poor Henry, my poor Henry, povero ...'

I don't know whether he says this because of my ruined garden or because of Louise. I'd happily disappear down a rathole, I'd drag Louise down there with me and strangle her with one hand, my hands are powerful claws, watch out.

Romeo has his fists on his hips. It's on account of the smashed greenhouse that he's lamenting. I'm relieved.

'My God, Henry, it's so difficult to look after tillandsias, and you had three of them! And your aeonium? It takes them fifteen years to reach that size.'

He paces up and down the garden, Elizabeth at his heels, he takes stock of the damage, his commentary is confused, he's speaking in Italian now, a threnody of misfortune. I'm overwhelmed, he is proof of the true scale of the disaster, he takes in his trembling hands severed stalks and lacerated leaves, my spectators have risen from their seats, they listen and follow him at a respectful distance, for his finale he takes in his left hand a smashed pot wherein lie the remains of a beloperone guttata, which I, for the sake of simplicity, call a prawn plant. He raises his head, he shakes the fist of his right hand menacingly in the direction of the prison wall, he begins

44

railing against the mutineers, he calls them savages, godless and lawless Mamelukes and Austrians. I must calm him down at all costs.

'Ssssh! Sssssh! Stop, Romeo, please! There'll be reprisals, they'll start throwing stuff again.'

'Paper flowers to apologize? Paper flowers! Don't you see how vulgar that is, Henry?'

'But I find it beautiful!' protests Louise. 'And what skill it takes to make them!'

At this moment, as though someone has pressed a button somewhere, a chorus of whistles comes from the upper windows of the prison. Bare arms emerge from between the bars, a new banner is unfurled, the words are written in green on a plastic yellow background. I read: NO FLOWERS FOR BLAIN, THE TORTURER COOK! Romeo is as blind as a bat, he asks Elizabeth to read out what is on the banner, I want to gag her, to knock her senseless, to . . .

'No flowers . . . for Blain, the torturer cook!'

I must be almost as white as my shirt. Charles grabs a chair and slips it under me. I feel faint, I sit down, it's like being knifed in the back.

'What does that mean?' Romeo stutters. 'They . . . they must have telly in the prison, they recognized you! Holy Mother of God, they recognize you from the news! You were on two nights in a row, weren't you?'

'I just don't understand it! What treachery! Someone's trying to get at me. We're never in direct contact with the prisoners, I never serve the food, I don't see how they could have recognized me.'

'But recognize you they did!' Elizabeth quips helpfully.

Distress invades me like a canker, it gets into the marrow of my bones, I shiver like a man badly wounded.

'It's slander!' shouts Romeo. 'You should sue them! Do these savages know where you live? But of course, the spokesman for the local people! Imagine if they manage to work out which your garden is. It'd be like Dresden in forty-five!'

Everybody stops speaking, as though for a minute's silence. I get up off the chair and take refuge in the kitchen. I take three aspirins with another glass of brandy, which I down in one. In the garden there's a confab about the slogan and perhaps also about my fate, my future, my destiny. I feel hatred rising in me, I demand the death penalty for these mutineers!

They finally leave. Elizabeth and Romeo keep repeating.

'Poor Henry! Christ have mercy on you, my poor Henry!'

Charles mimes the same sentiment with his rubber face. Their lament is becoming intolerable, I want them to clear off.

'I'll help you rebuild everything,' Romeo vows, 'I'll make some cuttings for you, you're not alone in your time of trouble, Henry.'

When I open the door to let them out I come face to face with a group of six people, all sent by Suzan to see the show. Romeo takes me by the elbow and leads me aside.

'You're not going to let another six pairs of eyes, another six witnesses see that villainous slander!'

We're almost in the middle of the street, we turn to face the prison – the top floor and the roofs are visible above the houses on the right. The banner can be seen over the houses near the administrative entrance.

'You see, Romeo, it's all the same whether they pay for a place in my garden or stay in the street. I might as well make a bit of money out of it, it'll help repair the damage when it's all over.'

I rejoin the group of visitors on my doorstep and ask them to wait a few minutes. Romeo's visit has certainly disrupted my little business. I check my ticket stubs and notice that three of the RARs should've been gone a good half hour ago. They thank me effusively for their very informative time on my premises and take their leave without a grumble. Which leaves two more who still have fifteen minutes each, I realign the chairs on my terrace, add another chair from the kitchen, and seat the new lot after pocketing sixty pounds. I'm so wound up, the lags have humiliated me, Romeo has vexed me, Louise has disgusted me. If I knew her better I'd have taught her a little lesson, even if she did have three glasses of brandy too many inside her. But I had to contain myself, remain courteous and smiling. Louise was thirsty, she wanted me to pour her a fourth glass, she was all languid and had a vague smile on her face, she wasn't aware of the gravity of the situation, she was staring into her glass as though there were shoals of phosphorescent jellyfish in it.

'He's a bit of a ninny, your "great gardener", Henry.'

I don't reply, and drain my fifth glass. Louise points her finger at the ceiling, she asks to see the flower-strewn street from upstairs, to get a better overview and take some photos. I reply drily that there are television reporters in the attic but that the view from my bedroom is just as edifying. On the stairs, I manage to keep calm when she leans on me for support. From my bedroom window it looks like a street party after the war or after a flower-decked float has passed to mark daffodil day in London, or after the historic peace of 1485 between the houses of York and Lancaster, with their white and red roses. Hundreds and hundreds of flowers make the road vibrate with warm colour under the low sky looming with black clouds. Louise seems to wake up at the sight. She takes photographs, leaning against the window ledge, her bust jutting out of the open window.

'You'll fall, Louise! Let me hold you.'

I've slipped my hands under her blue jacket, I place them on her soft, round hips. Another inch and I'll have her buttocks against my thighs, my anger has dissolved like sorbet in the sun, fever rises from my stomach. Louise lets my hands rest on her waist, she's framing her shot artistically. I have tender thoughts about our national flag. Then comes what sounds like a clap of thunder. Perhaps a bomb has exploded in Strangeways, two or three flashes light up the sky. Louise springs back, I almost tumble over the armchair at the end of my bed. Rain begins to fall, thick, heavy, suddenly freshening the air, like a storm at the end of summer, coinciding with another charge on the prison by the forces of order. From beyond the walls of the gaol, we hear, very distinctly, the sound of tear gas grenades going off, shouts, heavy boots on concrete, dogs barking. Curls of acrid smoke rise from a rooftop to our right, a helicopter appears above our heads, four men in riot gear standing at its open door. They throw into the prison yard and buildings smoke bombs that undoubtedly have the power to paralyze. I hear my spectators, three yards below me, giving little cries of: Oh, look! Look! and: It's the final assault! They're done for now! They're buggered! The rain falls with a rare violence, it forms little streams and large puddles on the broken tarmac, it drowns the flowers, carrying off a mush of faded paper. The street has been extinguished, the colours gone, the place is sinister once again, the stones and tar drab in the grey light. Tom and Jack move around in the attic, their nervous activity echoing through the ceiling. Three reporters charge into the bedroom, two of whom I've never seen before.

'How did you two get in?'

'Sorry. Jeff let us in. We're from *The Guardian* and . . .

'Look at the cut of you, you're completely out of breath and red as a herring! At your age I was haring up and down stairs and passageways in ships, and those stairs are steep, I can tell you. And I can still do it today! Anyway, you're very welcome. That'll be twenty pounds each.'

'We'll just take a few pictures and then we'll settle up.'

'Balderdash! It's cash up front. I'll give you your tickets and then you can take all the pictures you like, you can even go up on the roof if you fancy. But given the state you're in after the stairs, I wouldn't recommend it!'

I pocket the money, they pocket their blue tickets and continue their breakneck ascent to the attic.

'It's getting a bit out of hand here, Henry, don't you think? Maybe you should put a stop to it.'

'I'm technically unemployed, my dear Louise, in the past two days I've pulled in as much as I usually make in a week, now is not the time to give it up. Especially not with the weekend coming, the neighbours will be throwing open their houses too, there'll be a lot of competition. Come to think of it, I must go round and make sure they charge entrance fees as well, because if they don't the market will be ruined!'

'You're a scoundrel!' whispers Louise. 'In any case, the mutiny will be well over by the weekend and you'll be able to get back to your kitchens. But tell me, why are the prisoners being so horrid to you? What they wrote was really nasty!'

I don't know how to answer that. It was extremely bad luck that the lags had recognized me. Maybe it was one of the trusties who worked in the storerooms. Or maybe it was one of the prisoners who delivered the trays to the doors of the cells, a job which is a great privilege for any detainee. So they must've seen me, but I was always wearing my apron and my chef's hat. And I rarely spoke to them. The letters, money, razor blades, medicine and amphetamines that are hidden in the food are no concern of mine. I close my eyes, those are arrangements between my assistants, the screws and the lags, my hands are clean, all I do is cook. But the fact that one or more of the fifty odd mutineers recognized me from the telly is further proof that misfortune becomes me like a suit made to measure. So I merely sigh deeply and give Louise a distressed look. I fall once again into despondency. Ah, Louise, I no longer even have the leisure to desire you, my house is a hive which does not belong to me, people come, they go, they go up, they come down, no room is safe from their to-ings and fro-ings, I no longer dare put my hand on your bum.

'What's that, Henry?'

'I'm praying, Louise, I'm praying. That God may come to my aid.'

Louise feels sorry for me, I use the opportunity to invite her to dinner. She refuses, the afternoon is drawing to a close, she has to write another article for her rag, she wants to describe the flowery homage to the locals, to balance the piece she wrote yesterday. I make her promise not to mention the slanderous banner and place a kiss on her tender cheek. She says goodbye, I say I'll see her tomorrow. She smiles and runs off. The last rubbernecks and reporters leave soon after. Tom and Jack abandon their observation post at around six o'clock, bidding me an embarrassed farewell. My little house becomes silent and deserted.

Chapter IV

I felt very alone that Thursday evening, April 5th. I had no appetite at all, I ate fruit and cheese on crackers, washed down with port, raising each glass to Louise's health. I switched on the television to watch the news, thinking they would undoubtedly mention the latest skirmish in the prison. Strangeways was the second headline, the Home Secretary, David Waddington, made a brief appearance to declare that a further twenty-five mutineers had given themselves up and that the police, to whom he paid warm tribute, had regained control over the west wings of the prison. I leap from my sofa, I burst into rapturous applause, I dance for joy, yes! yes! yes! the kitchens have been liberated, the kitchens have been saved! Brendan O'Friel, the prison governor, appears and says the remaining mutineers, twenty or so of them, are now barricaded inside the south wings and no longer have access to the stocks of food, their surrender is thus imminent. Two BBC reporters were able to follow, cameras on their shoulders, the assault on the west wings, we see few pictures of the clashes, in fact we see very little, a bit of smoke, a few blokes running in the distance, a few stones being thrown. I don't recognize any of the courtyards, it could've been filmed anywhere except for the fact that the camera lingers on shots of the kitchens and the freezers, which, incidentally, don't look like the they've been damaged much, thank heaven. The presenter notes, however, that the reporters almost choked on the pestilential smell of fermenting vegetables and rotting meat and at the sight of sacks of rice and flour crawling with maggots and weevils. Which begs the question: how can the food stocks be in such a lamentable state after just five days of siege? To the poor living and hygiene conditions about which the mutineers have complained can now be added the worrying state of the food. The chief cook of the prison was personally implicated this afternoon by a new banner which the mutineers hung from the gaol's windows. Judge Tumin, the chief inspector of prisons, had, however, said in an official report in July 1989 that conditions at Strangeways were improving. A board of inquiry is to be set up ... I don't know what held me back, the fear of damaging my foot or of having to fork out for a new television, but I had the almost uncontrollable urge to put my boot through the screen. I hope they start stuttering, hiccoughing, that their faces become sinusoidal, these commentators spouting their bloody theories, and yes! wham! my foot landed in the padded side of the sofa, which didn't budge, absorbing the blow without hurting me. The only evidence was a trace of grey from my boot on the aniseed green material. I switched off the sluicegate of stupidity, now I understood Tom and Jack's embarrassed looks as they left. I hadn't thought about it while I was watching, but the shots could well have been taken from my place with a telephoto lens. That takes the biscuit, that villainous banner, as Romeo calls it. I drained what was left of my port and poured myself a large glass of brandy, I had sore need of it, cheers! Well they'll soon see what I'm made of if they carry on these attacks! I took the bottle and settled down on the sofa with the history plays and the Roman tragedies of my old friend Shakespeare. I was hoping to find an example of a character of the highest rank who finds himself in a perilous situation.

Everyone knows that the prison's electrical installations were damaged on the first day of the riot and that power to the freezers was probably cut off as early as Sunday afternoon. And it's common knowledge that frozen food, particularly meat and fish, must be cooked immediately once defrosted, if not, it begins to stink within a matter of hours. If one of my assistants forgets to close the fridge doors or if they cook defrosted food that's been lying around for too long, I have no choice but to throw a few cloves into the cooking pots in order to lessen the rather disagreeable smell. The prisoners have to be fed and the stocks are rigorously controlled, I'm not allowed to use more than a certain amount each day. All of which shows that frozen food that has been defrosted and left lying around for six days will pong! As for the waste that's left over after I've cooked the meat, it usually ends up being made into dog and cat food, a lorry comes to the prison once a week to pick it up, which brings in some money for our kitty. True, sometimes I do put bits of fat, or lungs, or intestines, or even gristle, into our powerful mincers, it makes for quite decent sausage meat which goes very well with beans. As for mutton bones, even if they are old and have had every bit of meat gleaned from them, they can provide a fine stock for soup or turnip stew. The commentators have no idea what they're talking about. One can never maintain control over a group of men, be they on board a ship or in a prison, if they're fed rotten food! Whether they are sailors you can no longer bear the sight of for having lived with them on the same boat for too many weeks, or pariahs, outlaws, worthless creatures who cost society far too much, I know from experience that you should never use the palate to mistreat them if the desire takes you to wreak some revenge or simply to carry out your own justice. Nobody's fooled by bad food, you can smell it a mile away, your nose needs to be of only average sensitivity to know from ten yards whether the food on the tray is edible or not. If it stinks, nobody wants it, what's on the plate ends up on the floor, on the walls of the cell, in the toilet bowl or in the face of the cook, who loses an eye or ends up with burnt and swollen cheeks. No. It always has to smell good and it has to be edible. You shouldn't aim for the palate, but target the stomach and the intestines instead. If they think they're eating royally but the long queue for the toilets moves so slowly that they must either defecate in their trousers or hang their bum over the ship's rail and shit into the sea, then the cook is jubilant, for he can claim the packaging of the food was faulty, he himself is above suspicion. How many times have I, as a cook on a merchant ship, made a show of rushing to the toilet while grasping my stomach, when in fact all I planned to do there was read Shakespeare and escape from the inane chatter of ailing and melancholy sailors. Thus they thought me of good faith, for they believed that I too was ill, and I was happy in this knowledge as I sat on my throne, calmly turning the pages as the truly sick hammered on the door and called out for me to hasten my movements. I would let them languish awhile, which added some spice to my undertaking, but it was impossible to read more than one or two pages, I could no longer hear the music of the lines. Some of the more desperate sailors ran ranting towards the toilets at the other end of the gangway, others fled up to the decks to release their ballast into the ocean, all cursed me wildly without knowing just how much I deserved their invective. I must point out that I've never acted gratuitously or without provocation. There has always been an insult, a threatening look, an arrogant mien, a way of showing that I am their flunkey, their punch-bag, and then bang! the next morning Montezuma has taken his revenge, as though the hand of God or perhaps the Devil has come to knead their guts until their stomach can be seen in

54

their faces, which take on the sweating and pallid aspect of sausage skin. To achieve this end I used strong magnesia-based laxatives which enabled me to target particular individuals without altering the taste of the food. It was only when I was on board the *Kaïnji* as she left Lagos and headed out into the Gulf of Guinea with a Liverpool-bound cargo of rubber and cotton – I was barely forty years old – that certain members of the crew got wind of my intrigues. They were Africans, of course, for Africans see spirits and witchcraft at every turn, but they didn't tell the captain. On the contrary, they expressed their deepest respect for me, they referred to me deferentially as the 'healer cook'. It was they who alerted me to the presence on board of an English passenger who was permanently drunk and never left his cabin, who sang, who howled, who screamed at a female spirit that haunted him but refused to speak to him. They beseeched me to introduce into the man's food a potion that would induce the woman from the beyond to leave the boat and find refuge in some marine altar, failing which we were all destined for a watery death. I responded to their prayers by lacing his food with powerful sedatives. I hoped that his silence would reassure them, but the passenger nourished himself only with cheap palm wine and never touched his meals. The female spirit, whose strength can only be described as out of the ordinary, thus came to embody for them the limits of my power. They were confirmed in their superstitious beliefs when the vessel caught fire in the Irish Sea; we were miraculously saved – with the exception of a young ship's apprentice who died of asphyxiation – by a tug from Liverpool that had been sent out to look for us. The Africans were the only ones who did not fall ill during the six-week journey, they took their meals together and I was able to spare them. They did, however, excite racist hatred among the other crew members, whose gurgling bellies had become their sole preoccupation, the clefts in their beleaguered buttocks worn by

55

a saffron diarrhoea that coloured the seats of their pants and opened up their anuses like camellias blossoming in pain. The poor Nigerians were regarded as devils whose dark entrails were as impervious to digestive troubles as their black skin was to the rays of sun. The racial animosity aboard the *Kaïnji* only served to fuel my jubilation. My Negroes eventually recognized the trap they had fallen into, and in the last two weeks of the crossing, they too began to fake severe visceral disruption. They clutched their stomachs and paraded their suffering with such drama that I could not help but admire them, we furtively wept with laughter whenever our paths crossed on a deserted gangway.

I'm drinking too much this evening. I can't concentrate on my reading of the second act of *Richard III*. It's not that I am nostalgic for those heroic years spent sailing the seven seas, I'm electrified by an avalanche of memories that crash down on me like a mute and terrible demand. I am far from finished! My life is proof! The telephone won't stop ringing even though it's late, perhaps it's my dear mother, but I shan't answer it. Tonight I'm alone and I raise my brandy glass to the future. When I think of the trip back from Chile on the big, blue, British-registered ore tanker, with its hold jammed with copper, when I recall that crew of useless bums and how, one night, they jostled and threatened me as I stood on the reardeck peacefully smoking my pipe and inwardly reciting the poetry of my only companion:

> His hand, that yet remains upon her breast, –
> Rude ram, to batter such an ivory wall! –
> May feel her heart-poor citizen! – distress'd,
> Wounding itself to death, rise up and fall,
> Beating her bulk, that his hand shakes withal.
> This moves in him more rage and lesser pity,
> To make the breach and enter this sweet city.

They reproached me for offering them pork for nearly all their meals, which wasn't anything to do with me, I hadn't received any orders from my superiors, they might as well be asking me for kosher or vegetarian food. The crossing was going to take eight weeks, which gave me plenty of time to prepare my response to these arrogant fools. This time I used lead-based astringents that contract body tissues and restrict secretions of body fluids. Constipation is ineluctable, regardless of the number of prunes one swallows. After five weeks of this diet, the villains no longer used the latrines, their bellies were as hard as rock. One could not approach them for their breath stank of the rocky depths of their guts, of their 'black souls', as I would say to anyone who cared to listen. Two overly superstitious Indian officers put them ashore at Pointe-à-Pitre, long before the end of the journey. With just three years to go before retirement, it was also my turn to be sent ashore even though the health authorities never found any evidence against me, despite carrying out two unannounced inspections in one year. Suspicion hung over my ability to regulate the sailors' stomachs, it had been noted in many captains' logs, the rumours had got as far as the maritime chambers of commerce in Liverpool. No charges were ever brought against me, but the only work I could get was on leaky old tubs carrying questionable cargoes. I went back to live with my mother in my home town, Liverpool, and it was by keeping an eye on the small ads that I landed myself the job in Manchester. The attention of the governor of Strangeways was drawn to the parallels he could see between life on a boat and in a prison, both enclosed spaces in which rebellion is called mutiny and the rebels mutineers. An icy smile cut across his face as he made the comparison. And that was that.

I fell asleep in the early hours, too drunk to make even the vaguest battle plan for the coming days. My face buried in the fourth scene of the third act of *Richard III*, in my sleep I slobbered over the page where Hastings bemoans the imminent loss of his head: *Yea, thou shalt be as he that lieth down in the midst of the sea, or as he that lieth upon the top of a mast.*

But what a fool he was too, so credulous and so sure of himself! Off with his head!

My mouth feels all furry, it's seven in the morning, the phone reverberates through my sore head, I'm too old to be having hangovers. It can't be Mother, she goes to bed early and never wakes up before nine; she stubbornly inserts her earplugs the instant she places her hearing aid on the bedside table.

'Did I wake you, Blain?'

'Good morning, Governor, to what do I owe the honour...'

'Can't you guess?'

'I...I did hear the good news, Governor, about the kitchens being recaptured. They've got no food left so they'll have to give in soon.'

'Didn't you hear what the journalists said about the food?'

'I did indeed, and pathetic it was too! Truly scandalous. But I'm not going to take it sitting down, I'm going to...'

'You're going to keep your mouth shut, Blain, that's what you're going to do. You've already done enough damage with your television nonsense. The prisoners weren't long in figuring out who the locals' spokesman was!'

'You mean that villainous banner?'

'There was no harm in showing another dimension of the havoc the prisoners are wreaking in the city. But public opinion swung over to their side after the flowers episode. Read the press, Blain, and you'll see! It'd give you something to do with all your leisure time. In short, if the media find out that this particular spokesman, who looks more like a war refugee, is none other than the chief cook, they'll say it's a government fix, won't they! So keep your head down, Blain. The only place I want to see you when this shambles is over is in the kitchens. And keep away from journalists until things settle down. If this business about the food gets any worse then we'll issue a public denial. But until then there will be no statement. You're highly dispensable, Blain, so don't tempt us!'

He slams down the phone. He clearly regards me as no more than a pawn on his chessboard; I don't really know what he meant by me being highly dispensable, and he wants me to keep away from journalists! That's a laugh, that one, they're like an occupying army here, I'm hardly going to pack my bags and head off on a fishing holiday somewhere along the banks of the Mersey! Besides, I can't just look the other way, it's a source of income, and one that could run dry tomorrow. This time my decision is made, I'll keep my head down all right! My only certitude at this moment is that I will do nothing, change nothing of my new life. But nevertheless, I have to recognize that today is not yesterday. Tom and Jack arrive at nine, they are distant, they display a forced politeness, as if to say: 'We're doing you the honour of using your attic, but we are not of the same world as you.'

'What about our time together in the war, doesn't that count for anything?' I ask point-blank.

They look everywhere but at me, they panic, they don't understand my remark, they smile nervously. I change my tone.

'Was it you who filmed that villainous banner yesterday, the one they showed on the news?'

'They were BBC pictures! They were filmed from the street!' they chorus, before disappearing up the stairs, relieved at having avoided the storm that hung in the air.

I open the French windows, I arrange the chairs on the terrace, the sky is blue, the April sun is gentle. I scan the horizon for that cursed banner and see, to my great consolation, that yesterday's fire has caused it to melt in parts. Now only the words FLOWERS and COOK can we made out. I give a whistle, bad luck has forgotten me. The Recommended or Anonymous Rubbernecks are still flocking to my home, most are customers from the pub, and many of the rest are their friends. Two turned up after strong encouragement from Romeo. My business is booming and I refrain from cleaning up the garden even though we're now, thanks to me, under the mutineers' protection. I've even gone as far as strewing a bag of rubbish, containing debris I'd gathered up at the risk of my own life on the second day of the mutiny, over the lawn and on certain flower beds.

'Hello, Henry, I hope we're not disturbing you. Suzan Carlos Simson sent us. Are there any places left?'

'Hello. Romeo Montague sent me. Is your garden still open for visits?'

This way, ladies and gentlemen, that'll be ten pounds each, the house is indeed open for visits, come and take the sun as you watch the prison, a performance is guaranteed! History advances slowly, but it advances inexorably. But the journalists are irritating and upsetting me now. For they turn up at my door and say they want to take pictures of the prison and I quickly realize that this is a pretext for snooping around my home and trying to engage me in conversation, that is if they don't come straight out and say: 'You are the head cook in Strangeways, aren't you? What do you think of the state of the kitchens? Were you surprised at the discovery of the rotting food? Why have the prisoners pointed the finger at you? Do you know that Justice Woolf is to lead a commission of inquiry into the mutiny? He's a staunch Catholic and is said to be incorruptible, heedless of pressure wherever it might come from. Does that worry you? The torturer cook, that's a bit strong, isn't it? After all, we've heard you carry out your duties conscientiously . . .'

The dogs! They prick me then they butter me up, they intimidate me then they comfort me. I'm very closely shaven, I can feel my eau-de-Cologne, the wave in my hair is impeccable. I've put on a tie over my checked shirt and over that a woollen V-necked jumper. I'm in my best slippers, the ones I wear on Sundays, the dark brown leather ones, I am the honest citizen who is being importuned in his modest suburban home. I have a fixed smile on my face and an insult on the tip of my tongue, I want to lash out when one of them takes the liberty of photographing me, but I keep my fists buried in my pockets, in one I grip my handkerchief, in the other my pack of cigarettes. I have no comment to make, I obey the governor, I express surprise that they should pay such attention to the crazed slogans of mutineers, stop! curtain! It is truly an ordeal, I'm exhausted by the end of the day and decide to go to Suzan's for a drink. After yesterday's clashes, today is a day of gentle repose, that's what a rather mannered old man told me, a chap who lives in a flat and who spent two good hours in the 'silence of History' here in the garden in very agreeable company. None of the prisoners has appeared on the roof, the police have not attempted another assault. There is a dead calm, it's as though the authorities wanted to make the world forget that Strangeways exists. More than 1,500 prisoners have by now been re-housed in other prisons, there is severe overcrowding, the Home Office is afraid that mutiny will break out in other penitentiary centres. At this time of the day I don't let anyone else in. I go upstairs to tell Tom and Jack I'm going out, they barely respond, sitting slumped over their equipment playing cards. I'd like to chuck them out too, but I made a deal with their producer that they can stay till Sunday.

I calm down as soon as I push open the door of the pub, I'm on home ground here. The smell of the beer that has impregnated the wooden tables, the cigarette smoke you could cut with a knife, the almost deafening chatter. I elbow my way to the counter, but Suzan is in the kitchen. I order a pint of mild and look for a seat. I should really keep reminding myself that my existence is incomplete if I do not come here every day. Some of the regulars have already spotted me.

'What's it like being famous, then, Henry?'

'Hello, Henry. Remember me? I was at your place when the police went in. Remember? The fire? The helicopter? The dogs barking? Crash, bang, wallop! And then that storm!'

They crowd around, listening, they're impressed by his story.

'Oh, yeah, you don't see the half of it on the telly. It's an entirely different matter if you're on the scene, isn't it, Henry? It's like news reports of a war, you're either there or you're not.'

'That's how it is in prison. You're either in or you're out. But if you're in, then you have to eat shit, apparently . . .'

His mocking smile, his wan face, his rasping voice, they annoy me. I get to my feet, the onlookers stand aside, I ask him just what he means. The smile disappears, his creased skin turns grey, he says he's seen terrible things on the television, that the prisoners are treated like animals . . . Suzan makes her way to the centre of the little group that has formed around the table, her hands are planted on her hips, she looks me in the eye, she frowns, she looks at the man, she asks if it's beer we're after because if it is the cellars are full of the stuff. Everyone smiles, the crowd disperses. I sit back down again, my legs have the shakes. I grab yesterday's copy of *The Sun* on the table, I try to appear composed, if I'm going to get harassed in Suzan's too I might as well throw in the towel. She bends over and speaks in my ear.

'Give me twenty minutes, Henry, and I'll come over and have a drink with you.'

I hold the paper wide open in front of me like a rampart. I

have an understanding neighbour at my table to whom I slip some money every time he goes up for a pint so that he can get me one too. I alternate between mild and Guinness, I read the paper line by line, I read everything; the business section, the ads, the sport, the latest antics of the royal family, the weather report. I'm bored silly, the beer is not helping, it's been three quarters of an hour and there's still no sign of Miss Carlos Simson. The place is emptying. I'm off. Suzan appears as I close *The Sun*, she has two pints in one hand and a stool in the other. She looks worried, she can't understand how I've managed to get myself mixed up in the whole situation.

'Is it true what they said about the kitchens, Henry?'

If she only knew what goes on in my kitchens. I take a pot that will hold one hundred rations. I pour in twenty kilos of bad white rice, I add forty litres of water, I add neither salt nor bay leaves, nothing! I cover and cook over a low heat. By the time the rice has absorbed the water it looks like white cement, it looks good, it almost shines. I might even have a little taste. There's the odd stone in it, but it does have a very pure rice taste, mushy and hard at the same time. It's not bad, it's not an insult to the palate, it's neutral, it's edible. I boil three turnips and the meal's ready. And on a bad day that's all I do. A bad day is a day when I'm in a foul mood, a day when I resent humanity, the humanity of whom I have not a deformed but a magnified view here in Strangeways. It's as though I'm seeing the world through a microscope: the hatred, the pettiness, the malice, the dirty tricks, the murders, the love, the friendship, the honour, the solidarity, the fear, the power, it's all so clear, so touchingly distinct. So I add neither salt nor bay leaves nor tomato sauce nor minced meat. I am a stone, I want their stomachs to become stone, I want them to shit stones. And I go on like this for a few days: rice, pasta, potatoes, pasta, potatoes, rice. Even if my good humour does return, I nevertheless try to complete the programme. But I can just as

63

easily cook split peas one day, cauliflower the next, beans the day after that, and on the fourth day Jerusalem artichokes – freezing permits one to provide a homogenous range in any season. I add bay leaves, salt, pepper, sometimes large onions, margarine and sausages that I've made myself. The taste is gratifying, it's well seasoned, it's fragrant, the trays always come back empty, but after seven or eight meals of this type, the bowels begin to speak. The gurgling starts, the belching, the farting, the backfiring, and this on the scale of 1,600 men in a confined space. The air echoes with millions of farts, short, long, deep, sharp, farts that come in volleys, dry, wet, a cannonade of all calibres. It's war, the sonorous air is filled with intestinal effluvia, it poisons the cells and the gangways. I know that the lags have an indulgent attitude to this sort of self-expression, and it's one I share on the days when my mood is gay. I like to use the detainees' entrails to make the atmosphere unbearably loud and unbearably smelly for the screws, to make them feel as though they have their heads stuck in the foggy seats of their prisoners' pants. During these periods the warders become nervous, irritable, aggressive, they lose their self-control, powerless as they are to control the quality of the air. I know a particularly sensitive screw, one nearing retirement, who has never hurt a fly and who found himself in the security business just as much by chance as one ends up in Her Majesty's navy. He walks around with a flask of lavender water in his back pocket, he has cotton buds which he dips into the flask and then sticks up his nostrils, alleging that they're for his frequent nose-bleeds. They call him 'Slow Bud' because no one has ever seen him run, whatever the situation. The cartilage in his nose and his face bones must be well marinated from the lavender water. Sometimes, with dull determination, alternating the dishes over four days, I cook lentils, kidney beans, broad beans, and Brussels sprouts. I often add mutton bones, minced meat or chicken wings which we buy in quantities of a hundred kilos at a time. And sometimes, as when I was cooking on the high seas, I add magnesia. These are not my days of foul humour, these are my days of great despair, when I have the irrepressible desire for humanity to end its days liquid, runny brown and putrid – thanks to the Brussels sprouts – in the bottomless pits of the toilet bowls. I want bowels to empty themselves of their diarrhoea, stomachs to empty themselves of their viscera, I want the world to become a browny black liquid and pour into the dark river in the incandescent centre of the earth, the place where the devil has his ovens. I, the head cook in Strangeways, know that the power I have over the bowels of my little collection of condemned men makes me omnipotent with regard to the air they breathe, the state of their flesh, the disposition of their spirit, and, finally, the plumbing, whether it be the tubes that run through the lags' stomachs or the pipes that line the penitentiary buildings. And I am the only one who knows, I am able to take the baseness of men's souls and extract its quintessence, but I can also make men gentle and pliant like a skin that has been soothed with some sweet-smelling lotion. The Lord's anointed as it is written of kings in historical dramas, I can cause a riot by suddenly changing the taste of the food I produce, I can clog up the plumbing and transform the prison into a multi-storey cesspit, no one knows just how mighty I am within my realm.

'What are you thinking about, Henry? Why don't you say something? So it's true, then?'

'Suzan, you know what it's like cooking for a lot of people. You don't really think, do you, that you can serve up just anything, even if they are prisoners?'

And I remind her that defrosted food goes off quickly and begins to stink immediately. I explain that the bits of meat that are left over go to make dog and cat food, I tell her of the miracles I must perform with seasoning in order to produce food fit for human consumption, despite Evans Norton's best efforts. I don't mention him by name, that swine who controls the stock, who will order any old rubbish, blithely ignoring all health and safety regulations, indifferent to the need to store food in proper conditions. All he is concerned with is staying within his budget and proving his administrative abilities. Suzan doesn't realize that I'd need to be like Jesus changing water into wine!

'But Suzan, I shouldn't really have told you that, so mum's the word, OK? You see, I'm not a complete bastard! If only you knew what goes into my dishes apart from food. Razor blades, knives, medicine, syringes, messages, sweets, even love letters! But I close my eyes to it all, Suzan. I close my eyes, if it brightens up their daily lives, then that's their business, I'm not going to play at being a screw.'

Suzan stares at me wide-eyed, she hasn't touched her beer. I drain my pint and start on hers. I tell her about a report I saw on the television one night. It was about a big Asian city, a Chinese city, where there is no mains drainage or treating of liquid waste, which goes straight into the earth. I wonder just how deep into the soil the evacuations of these millions of people go, do gases rise back up to the surface, are there virulent fermentations, are crops poisoned, is there land subsidence, do buildings cave in, does a fulminating stench rise up towards the heavens as though the earth was letting a gigantic fart. Since they are poor people who eat, like the prisoners, poor-quality food, their shit must be all the more fetid and shapeless, the soil, like their skin, all the more scrofulous. I imagine also that all these people who live and build on layers of shit, the more they build, the more the subsoil is fouled up. I think, I ask myself: could it not be that by emptying our bowels into the entrails of the earth we will end up extinguishing its fiery core? Will we end up filling the earth with shit until it explodes like an overfull septic tank, blasting us all into the sky in an ultimate deflagration?

'God, Henry! Why are you telling me all this? You're getting all mystic! Here, have the rest of my beer. I've got to get back to the bar. It hasn't done you any good, being on the telly.'

Chapter v

Louise is wearing a mouse-grey blouse, top buttons undone to reveal the smooth skin of her chest. When she leans over to talk to me, I see the edge of her champagne-coloured, lace, half-cup bra. But I'm anxious and depressed, I dare not bring my knee close to hers under the table. Our hands are sensibly placed on the white tablecloth, the light is gentle and golden. I cannot make out her eyes, the flame on the candle is reflected in her glasses, it makes her look like a will-o'-the-wisp. We're in a French restaurant, right in the centre of Manchester, very near the Royal Library, it was Louise's idea to come here, she's mad about 'French gastronomy'. The food is expensive, the wine exorbitant. I'm technically unemployed, but it's our first dinner together so I moan only to myself. The starter was exquisite: venison terrine on a bed of warm redcurrants for me, vol-au-vents in prawn sauce for Louise. Afterwards we devoured cod with a very buttery and creamy sauce normande, now I await my entrecôte vigneronne, if you don't mind, Louise her tournedos à la moelle; there are a lot of sauces in French cuisine . . .

'In bourgeoise cuisine, Henry!'

She's a bit tight-lipped and haughty, which irritates me. I refill our glasses with Saint-Émilion, which takes my mind off her failings. I can see the evening is not propitious for attempting the conquest of Louise. She's shown me her article on 'the Strangeways mutineers who deck the town with flowers', it's a passionate text on the prisoners: like all human beings, they have a store of goodness within themselves and were able to present their excuses in the form of flowers, despite the risks they had to run to get out on the slippery roofs. I feel that she's distrustful of me, she suddenly declares over the plates of steaming meat:

'I was shocked by what I saw on the telly, Henry. The state of the kitchens! Was there some truth in that banner?'

I was about to lift the first forkful of my entrecôte to my lips, the vigneronne sauce was dripping on to the plate. Louise doesn't seem at all bothered about ruining my appetite, she's looking down at her food, she's slashing at her tournedos. I'm exasperated, the meat trembles at the end of my fork. Louise looks up and meets my frozen stare.

'I didn't mean to annoy you, Henry, I thought I was getting to know you a little, you ... you seem so considerate beneath your gruff exterior. I just want to understand what was going on, that's all.'

So I describe the kitchens, what it's like to have to cook for a horde of people. I tell her about Norton, about the broken fridges, about how the food has been defrosted since Sunday, about the offal that goes into dog and cat food, I hear her murmur 'poor things'. As I chew on my stringy entrecôte, I even tell her about the cities in China that are built without any proper sewage systems. Unlike Suzan, Louise agrees with my apocalyptic vision of the container and the contents.

'That's our ... earthly side. Fortunately we compensate for this gravity that is constantly pulling us towards the bottom ...'

'The bottom, yes ...'

'I'm not joking, Henry! We compensate for it by a pure,

upward movement of the soul that carries us towards the heavens and towards God!'

'You're absolutely right, I . . .'

'Don't you see? Even these so-called dregs of society, these pariahs, their first act in the mutiny was to climb onto the roof! As if . . . as if they were waiting for a sign from God.'

Louise thinks she has understood me, she's convinced by my arguments, she's reassured, she softens.

'This tournedos is so tender!'

She smiles again.

'You're a great comfort to me, Louise. It's so trying to be dragged through the mud by the press. They write such rubbish.'

'You know, Henry, if you hadn't left a message, I wouldn't have phoned you. I was just too shocked.'

I nearly hadn't phoned her. I'd got back from the pub with my head full of black thoughts after Suzan walked off and left me sitting there in front of her pint of Guinness. I dialled Louise's number feverishly, the answering machine sprang into action, but before the beep came church music followed by a hymn, the organ vibrated, the voices became hoarse, the earpiece of my phone was saturated with noise. It lasted an interminable minute. I was discouraged by this telephone religiosity – it had already been enough of an effort to bring myself to call her, I would only be able to stutter into the phone. There hadn't been any sign of Louise all that Friday. I'd said 'see you tomorrow' as she was leaving the previous evening, she'd looked at me with tenderness in her eyes, which I read as acquiescence, ah, Louise, I felt like hanging up . . . 'Hello, this is Louise. Here? Not here? What does it matter? Speak after the beep and I'll get your message . . . Beep!'

'Hello? It's Henry, Henry Blain. Hi, Louise. Well, looks like you're not at home. OK, give me a call sometime. Talk to you soon, I hope. Bye ... it's ... it's Henry.'

I hung up. I hate talking to machines. If I'd been calling her after slitting my throat with my hedge-cutters I'd have bled dry like a stuck pig before I even got to say hello or goodbye or help. I'll tell her one day that her church music sets my nerves on edge, but now is not the time for discourteous remarks. The phone rang ten minutes after I left the message. I jumped to answer it, it was the governor's secretary. Miss Smith told me that an official denial was about to be made to the press regarding the state of the kitchens, which had become the subject of much controversy. Some commentators were now saying that we mixed cat and dog food into the food served to the prisoners. The governor wanted to hear my views on the matter. These I gave her, but I omitted to say that proceeds from the sale of meat leftovers went into a slush fund. She listened attentively, advised me, as a 'friend', to keep out of sight in the coming days, then hung up, the bitch. She's as thin as a rake, she thinks she's the bee's knees because Sir Brendan O'Friel dictates letters to her. I went out for a stroll in the garden and twisted my ankle on a brick. I swore like a trooper and sat down to rub my poor foot. As I looked up I was sure I saw, through the darkness, some figures walking on the prison roof. The night air was mild, soon I was certain I could see the glow of cigarettes on the ridge of one of the roofs. What ideas had they got in their heads, these stubborn mutineers? What did the poor devils dream of? What did they hope to gain by holding out for a few extra hours? I just wanted everything to get back to normal, I wanted the prisoners back in their cells, the warders in their guard rooms, and me in the kitchens. Louise phoned half an hour later, she let herself be persuaded, but she was not enthusiastic.

'OK, why not? If you'd like that ...'

She gave me the address of a restaurant called Made in France. I didn't argue, I was on my best behaviour.

The Coulommiers cheese is excellent, we drink the second bottle of Saint-Émilion, we enjoy our îles flottantes. It is as though we are paying homage to our beautiful country, I venture. Louise laughs wildly, she has tears in her eyes. I take the opportunity to grasp her knee between mine, she does not resist. I order two glasses of Napoleon brandy, my day's profits are about to be swallowed up by the bill, I've never spent as much on a meal, but Louise is purring like a cat in the sun, I'm already beginning to feel more of a man.

She lives fifteen minutes walk from the restaurant; I walk her home, she says she had a lovely evening, she is reconciled. I take her arm as we cross the road, her gait is languid, she can't walk in a straight line, she bursts out laughing on several occasions, she throws back her head, she says: 'Look – there's a grille around the bulb on the lamppost!' and she laughs until she gets the hiccoughs. I look at the lamppost, I force a smile, we carry on our way. We arrive at a modest development of three redbrick blocks around a courtyard with a large chestnut tree in the middle, and stop at a stairwell that stinks of cat piss. Louise thinks I shouldn't go any further.

'I'll manage the two flights of stairs on my own, Mister Chef!'

She roars with laughter, salutes me, and trips on the first step. I catch her, clasp her around the waist, steal a kiss from her lips, she sets off again up the stairs, she sings 'Yellow Submarine', her head nodding, she'll wake up the whole building. I hear her slam her door and am piqued but still upbeat, tomorrow is another day, as Mother says. I jump on a bus that brings me home, I am a young man again, I whistle 'Yellow Submarine', at ten past eleven I push open the door of my house, slip on my slippers, I'm home. I make myself a cup of tea, I switch on the television – it must be a programme about the circus, I see a bald man with a beard, bare-chested, holding a set of dumbbells above his head, but instead of weights on each side, there are young women in sequined bikinis perched on bicycles. The man's face is violet red, his powerful body trembles, crash! he drops everything. The bicycles tumble, the beautiful blonde ejected from her saddle falls to the ground, the beautiful brunette wobbles on her bike, the man, now flat on his back, is choking, the presenter rushes towards him, calls the first aid team, he looks panicked, it's a real live heart attack. The blonde has broken her ankle, she can't get up, she sits there with her legs wide apart, vey erotic, the brunette has buried her head in her hands, her round breasts are bursting out of her bikini top, they rise and fall with each sob. The first-aider sets up a ventilator, a doctor arrives on the scene, the cameras remain glued on the dying strongman, on the blonde's thighs and the brunette's breasts, what a circus!

The phone rings. I answer it, certain that at this time of night it can only be Louise.

'Louise?'

'It's your mother. Henry! Who's Louise? Is that why I haven't been able to get through to you for the last two hours? Are you going to get married again?'

'Hello, Mother, how are you?' I answer.

'Did you see the news? Of course you didn't, you were with your lady love. She's a smart one! I wanted to talk to you yesterday after what they said about you . . .'

I see four ambulance men running onto the set with two stretchers. They put the beautiful blonde on one, she grimaces, her ankle is giving her a lot of pain. The beautiful brunette pulls at her hair and claws at her chest, one of her breasts has popped out from her bikini, the nipple glistens under the studio lights, she groans, she snivels.

'I'd hoped you would answer them on the telly, you know. They want to drag the Blains into the gutter, that's what they want.'

With much difficulty, for he is heavy, they place the old weightlifter on the other stretcher.

'And this evening your governor was interviewed. "We do our utmost to ensure the prisoners get decent food" – that's what he said.'

He's laid out on the stretcher. The ambulance men barely manage to lift it, they stagger under the weight, the thinnest one looks very shaky, he looks like he's going to have a coronary himself, the presenter commentates as though the whole thing were a sports event, the ambulance man at the front stumbles, the one behind has to run so as not to drop the stretcher.

'And he also said, and I quote: "If there is a lame duck among the kitchen personnel, the commission of inquiry will find him. There should be no doubt that we will take all the measures necessary." Who is it, Henry, this lame duck? Is it you? Do they want to make you carry the can?'

'The billycan?'

Suddenly the heart-troubled weightlifter pulls off his oxygen mask, he gets up on his elbows, he opens his eyes, smiles at the camera and gives the viewers a big wave. The stretcher-bearers zigzag off, the audience applauds.

'It was a joke, Mother, a joke!'

'You'll be laughing on the other side of your face in no time if you let them walk all over you like that. Stand up for yourself, for God's sake! Think of your father, your brother, think of me! I can't go out any more for fear of meeting the neighbours, now that my son's been branded a torturer. Fight your corner, your mother's counting on you. Bye, love.'

She hung up. I had felt the rage taking hold of her, her tone had become abrupt, she preferred to stop the conversation short rather than end up barking into the phone. I'm disconcerted and vaguely bitter.

The old strongman and the two young women wave goodbye to the audience, the presenter is exultant, the switchboard, he says, is about to explode with the number of calls from viewers, some of them, in shock, thought the weightlifter was dead and had said goodbye to the world in a last convulsion. This gruesome programme, which was not about the circus after all, is a triumph. I see from the credits that it's called 'A Family Evening'. I go to bed.

Tom and Jack traipsed into my room this morning while I was still in bed. I was drowsily reading the paper. I gave a start when I saw them at the foot of my bed, Jack in his black leather jacket and Tom in his loden coat, bringing the cold in with them.

'Have you come to arrest me?' I muttered.

They smiled.

'The news doesn't have a lie-in at the weekend, more's the pity,' sighed Tom.

And they went on their way. I found them less distant towards me than yesterday, I felt like a lord in bed, propped up on my white pillows, in my lovely plum-coloured, green-striped pyjamas. Then it sank in that journalists did indeed work weekends and that I hadn't been to see my neighbours to tell them the going rates. I jumped out of bed and threw on some clothes, gave myself a close shave and splashed on some eau de cologne. Seven houses offered roughly the same view of Strangeways as my own. The gardens of four of them had disappeared, the tenants having built in a rather slapdash manner a shower room, the second toilet, a kitchen extension, kennels made out of reinforced concrete, hen-houses, sheds made from breeze-blocks or corrugated iron in which they worked on mopeds, made kitchen furniture, kept spare parts which hadn't always become spare of their own accord. These gardens had become dumping grounds where the tenants did their DIY in the evening or at weekends to put a little bit more meat on their tables, it was impossible to get anywhere near the lane that runs along the prison wall. But there were still the windows, and I preferred to let everyone know that the journalists might turn up, that they had to charge at least twenty-five pounds to newspaper reporters and fifty to television people, which was around twenty per cent higher than my own rates. I didn't want to lose the customer base I had worked so hard to acquire.

On the whole I have good relations with my neighbours. I am perhaps the most notable person on the estate on account of my fine garden, the fact that I have the outside of my house painted every five years, and because of my position as the head cook in the prison. How often have they asked me to tell them of the sordid goings-on inside Strangeways so they can frighten their children, half of whom are on the road to delinquency. As I love telling stories, I have become the narrator of Strangeways atrocities. I've told them of the gang wars, of the need to choose which side you belong to, of the gang bosses who carve up the jail between them and who live like lords as they rule over 1,600 souls, of the rackets, the settling of scores, some of which have been ordered from outside the prison, the prostitution, the suicides, the drugs, the young offenders who go inside for stealing a car and who come out junkies. My listeners shiver when I go into detail about the sophisticated executions, the mutilations, the rapes, the state of the injured when they're brought to the infirmary under the mocking eyes of the screws. The parents listen to me, alarmed, the adolescents display unhealthy curiosity – I see in their eyes the deep-seated desire to go to the bad. I've no need to invent anything, I just have to keep my ears open, the kitchens are like a crossroads, the trays serve just as much to collect information as to distribute food. But none of the stories I so tastefully recount, and which have earned me many a beer in almost every house on the estate, has set a single teenager back on the straight and narrow, and I've lost any influence I once might have had over my audience. We remain on polite terms, we exchange a few words about the rain, but I don't have the courage to ask after Simon, Paul, Ann, Matthew, Alicia, they're all between thirteen and twenty, and their future is far behind them if I'm to judge from the frequent visits by the police.

I was well received at all the doors upon which I knocked. They thanked me for speaking up on their behalf on the television, some of them were hoping to be able to claim on their insurance, it was a godsend really that their rotten, patched-up roofs were half-destroyed at the height of the riot, they should be able to get them repaired or even get new ones put in thanks to my comments on ITV. They all agreed to charge the journalists. Old O'Connor, a boilermaker, who has, in the shed that occupies his entire garden, a veritable scrap yard of mechanical objects, cast iron and sheets of rusting metal, who is the father of six children and the husband of a drunkard of a wife, and who has only two windows that would be of any use to reporters, gave me a rather laboured wink and asked if we couldn't agree to charge higher prices.

'Why not, David,' I replied. 'Once we agree on a minimum entry fee. You're right, we shouldn't let them screw us. Just think how much they sell their pictures for.'

I clenched my fist and shook it in the air.

'We won't let them take advantage of us, David!' I added.

A big smile came over his badly shaven, ashen face. He offered me a whisky. Poor old O'Connor, this particular neighbourhood deal won't bring him a single penny. His Scotch is excellent. Cheers.

I don't know what intuition it was that made me put off my

visit to the Bushys', but as every house had so far been welcoming, and as the many beers and shorts I'd imbibed over the course of the morning had emboldened me, I decided to finish my tour with a knock on number three. Peter Bushy's thirty-tonne truck was, as was sometimes the case at the weekend, parked in front of his house, half on the pavement and half on the pot-holed street. When the trailer is attached, the lorry stretches beyond the perimeters of the Bushy garden, partially obstructing the views from the front windows of numbers one and five, which appears not to bother anyone. I waited a good two minutes before I heard his slippers over the cement floor of his hall. He's dressed, as always, in blue overall bottoms and a sleeveless vest, also blue. He's half bald and has a weak chin, accentuated by his thick black moustache; he's small, neckless, stocky and muscular like an ancient Greek wrestler. He opened his door with such vigour that I thought I'd be sucked up into an air pocket, the smell of his cigarillos and his bitter perspiration assailed me. He said a distracted hello as he sucked on his little cigar, I asked him to forgive me for disturbing him, he didn't react, and simply looked at me. When I explained the situation, his face turned chalk-white. I didn't see his hand coming for me, he grabbed the back of my imitation suede jacket, I heard the buttons of my checked sports shirt being ripped off, my feet lifted off the ground, the odour of his armpits was suffocating. He carried me down the hall and into the living room and dropped me by the French windows. I saw a garden filled with tyres. Tractor tyres that served as tubs for shrubs and rose trees, there were jardinières that had two or three levels depending on how the tyres were piled and how big they were, there were pyramids – bases made of lorry tyres that tapered up towards the summits of Austin Mini tyres – the height of a man planted with miniature pine trees. In one corner planted with begonias I recognized an arrangement of scooter and pram tyres that

78

resembled a mosque, the minarets formed by shell fragments from the last war. All the edge of the paths were lined with tyres cut in two or four, it looked like a go-kart transformed into an ornamental garden. He pointed out the three press photographers installing their tripods, today again there was talk of a final assault. Here in Bushy's garden we were just under a new banner that had been put up this morning: BISCUITS & CHOCOLATE FOR 100 YEARS. NO SURRENDER! I thought about the stocks in the screws' canteen, where there must indeed be quantities of biscuits, beer, chocolate and tea. Bushy screamed at me.

'Here, they get in free whether they're from the telly or the papers. I want the world to see the fight the lads are putting up inside there, and what those bastard cops are up against, trying to get them out. You're some fucker, it ain't enough for you to starve them with your rotten food, you wanna make money on their backs as well! So scarper! Go on, get the fuck out of here!'

I recalled that Bushy had a son in prison in Leeds. I glimpsed furtive smiles on the faces of journalists, I recognized one who had been in my place the day before yesterday. Again my feet left the ground, I did the same journey in the opposite direction, Peter Bushy ejected me like a load of dirty laundry, I desperately tried to regain my balance as I flew over the four yards of gravel before the open gate. I went through it and my flight came to a halt at a wheel of his lorry, my head made contact with the rubber and I collapsed on to the ground. I was stunned, I sat down in a puddle of fuel oil, my neck ached.

'If I was ten years younger you'd be dead meat, Bushy,' I muttered at his closed door.

I rubbed my neck, I looked up and saw his new wife looking down at me from their curtainless bedroom, holding a white poodle in her arms. She was wearing a black bra, I could see tattoos on her bare shoulders, she had raven black hair with green streaks that looked like antennae, she had a ring stuck through her lower lip and she was smoking a fat cigar, she's fifteen years younger than Peter, she's much amused by my rout. I thought of Mary, Bushy's first wife, she was entirely different, tall, slender, bleached blonde hair falling down over her shoulders, firm and full breasts, she dressed like a real woman. I saw her in the supermarket car park one scorching day in July 1986, she was about to walk home, she was pulling her overflowing little trolley along behind her, her feet clad in leopard-skin high heels, her bum poured into a pistachio green miniskirt. I followed her, magnetized by her figure, and three hundred yards further along, in the midday sun, her trolley lost a wheel and her tins of dog food, her crackers and her sausages went flying. Like the Good Samaritan that I am, I rushed to help her pick up the objects strewn across the footpath, I goggled at the curve of her breasts tucked inside her flesh-coloured bodice, snug between her thighs I could make out her brown-haired pussy lying unfettered by underwear, the axle of the wheel was broken, it was irreparable. We were no more than five minutes from our street, so I offered my services. I lugged the heaviest bags, the ones with the bottles and tins, Mary talked about the weather, about her son, on holiday with his grandparents in the country, about Peter, her husband, who was doing very nicely, thank you, who was in the international haulage business, must be somewhere between Turkey and Iraq at the moment, she added with a cannibalistic smile. Ah, I cried, I know what it is to travel to the four corners of the earth. My face was dripping with sweat, I was a little out of breath.

'Come in for a minute, Mister Blain. I'll give you a nice cool glass of orangeade, you deserve it.

We are in the kitchen, Mary is squatting by the open fridge, I pass her the contents of the bags, her bodice is too short, it reveals her lower back, I'd be happy to sit here all day taking stuff out of supermarket bags, since each time I had over a bottle of milk, a piece of Gouda, a packet of sausages wrapped in plastic, four yoghurts, a bag of lemons, I get a little closer to her . . . That's it! My right hand is riveted to her waist, I stroke her hips even though I still have a tray of plums in my left hand. Mary sighs, now both her knees are on the tiled floor, she supports herself with one hand on the fridge door, the other no longer waits to receive food, I feel it groping between my legs in search of my flies, which she soon finds and unbuttons with the dexterity of the visually impaired. I have an enormous hard-on, I throw the plums into the vegetable compartment, I pull her skirt up over her waist, I discover the splendour of her broad, pale buttocks. She clasps me firmly in her ringed hand, and leads me resolutely towards her wooded mons Veneris, her crotch swallows my cock, such warmth, Mary, truly this is a monsoon. 'Come on, Henry, come on!' I don't know which of us says it, but we rock back and forth in concert, we do it doggie-style, the fridge purrs as it vainly tries to refrigerate the victuals piled on its shelves. I see her quivering, creamy bum, her arched back, her shoulders, her blond neck, the bottle of milk, the cans of beer, the Emmenthal, the jar of gherkins, the sliced bacon, the eggs, the entire edifice tinkles and trembles, and Mary's right hand hunts nervously in the freezer compartment for ice cubes, come on, Henry, come on! She grabs a handful, rubs them over her breasts, come on, Henry, come on! Oh, Mother, yes! Yes! The delft cat and the wooden cuckoo clock that were on top of the fridge come crashing down at the crucial moment, they lie in pieces on the tiles. Mary doesn't care, she fixes her skirt and her bodice.

'You don't act your age,' she tells me with a half smile.

We drank a lot of orangeade laced with vodka as we played Scrabble on her Formica table. After this first little test of hers to see if I was still vigorous, we were to meet regularly in her kitchen over the course of a year. I was, however, always a little bothered by the presence of her German shepherd, who sat in its basket in a corner of the kitchen and observed our noisy frolics. Mary would groan and give raucous cries while her dog whined with excitement at the spectacle or perhaps at our smell. Several times I put him out into the hallway, but he knew how to open the door. One day I jammed a chair against it but he made such a racket – he growled, he yapped, he scratched frenziedly at the wood – that I went soft. Mary started moaning in frustration.

'What's wrong, darling, have you got myxomatosis or something?'

'Shit! It's your bloody dog that's put me off!'

'Poor Ace! My little treasure.'

So I had to put up with the presence of the German shepherd with the lubricious look in his eye, tongue hanging lasciviously out of the side of his mouth. I was always afraid he'd take advantage of my distraction and take a chunk out of my backside, my attention entirely devoted as it was to the burning body of this bottle blonde, who had the appetite of an ogress and who would leap on me with a desire that brooked no delay, scattering the Scrabble letters all over the kitchen, a little vexing as it invariably happened when the score was very close and the game nearly over. Her vocabulary was quickly enriched by our linguistic jousts and soon I could no longer beat her as easily as in the first weeks of our cavorting. And it was often disconnected by her habit of leaving me, dick waving aimlessly in the air, to go and fetch a bowl of ice cubes she'd left in the freezer earlier. She'd place the bowl within arm's length before returning my quivering member to the depths of her large, warm and hospitable vagina. Her fingers fiddled with the ice like a nun with the beads of her rosary, she then began to rub them over her breasts, which was an early sign that we were at the gates of heaven. If she was astride me this unfortunately meant that icy drops of water would fall onto my stomach. One day, she must've been in a particularly generous mood, she decided she wanted to stroke my sternum. I was underneath her and leapt up in fright, nearly sending her flying head over heels. Luckily we were on the ground, she managed to get her hands on the floor and regain her balance, but she had knocked over the cleaning stuff stored under the sink, overturned the rubbish bin and crashed into the bottles of oil and wine lined up against the wall.

'Christ!' she cried as she sat among the bottles rolling around on the floor like skittles, 'You rammed it in so far it was almost coming out my mouth.'

Mary often had to use her skilful hands and mouth to rekindle me, for I am so very sensitive to the cold and am easily put off the business at hand, which I obviously regard as a pleasure but also as a very serious matter. I thus preferred to take her from behind, over the Formica table, which was very stable on its metal legs, even if the ice cubes did end up wetting the Scrabble board. At least I was shielded from the melting ice and Ace's jaws.

Our little slap and tickle and Scrabble sessions came to a sorry end on the second of May the following year. Peter Bushy drove his thirty tonnes past my house and made the walls shake. He was off to Poland after a long week at home. I couldn't contain myself any longer, I ran down the back lane, the one that skirts the prison wall, and pushed open the gate, which at the time opened onto a weed-infested garden with a Christmas tree planted in the middle and a washing line stretched from end to end. I could see Mary's immense, abundant white arse everywhere, on the pavements, in the streets, in the windows of the houses, I had a lump in my throat and a cock so hard it hurt.

I open her back door silently and tiptoe in. I stop at the living room door, I hear groans, I see that louse of a dog, its eye fixed and gleaming, its maw hanging open, its tongue longer than ever, and under it, stretched out on the pale green carpet, like Romulus and Remus between the paws of the she-wolf, is Mary, stark naked, on her back, legs spread. But she isn't sucking at the German shepherd's teats, she's giving the hound a hand job with her expert hand, she moves it gently back and forth, regular as clockwork. Her eyes are closed, she pants expressively, massaging her pussy with her other hand, index finger on her clitoris. I grab the large, heavy vase they store their umbrellas in and smash it with all my strength over the skull of the dog, who is so concentrated on his sexual pleasure that he has not reacted to my presence. The sound of the blow is muffled, dull, dense. The beast's eyes cloud over. Ace drops dead, he lands on his mistress's breasts, she writhes beneath him, she doesn't know what's going on, her respiratory tracts are almost blocked by the dog's coat. I slam the doors of the living room and hall behind me, and go home, mad as a bull, Mary is not a respectable woman. I haven't even put on my slippers when the phone rings.

'You bastard! You fucking bastard! I'm going to call the police!'

'And I'm going to call the vice squad!'

I hang up, that's quite enough of that. An image haunts me all afternoon: Mary, Ace and I in the same crumpled bed sheets. The image is called 'The Three Of Us'.

After dark I hear tapping at the kitchen window. I open the back door. It's Mary, wrapped in a long black coat, her lips smeared with red lipstick, her eyelids excessively painted but not enough to conceal the fact that she's been crying all afternoon. I close the door behind her, her coat swings open to reveal a purple négligé, high heels push her up to my height, her legs are in black stockings held in place by suspenders, her mons Veneris is unclad, she's perfumed herself with a flowery spray. With one hand she clasps my neck, with the other she undoes my flies, her tongue explores the crevices of my ears, pushes itself inside my mouth, slides over my teeth, caresses my gums, her breasts, her throat are irresistible magnets.

'Were you jealous, darling, you cranky little thing, you?'

I push her away, I punch her in the stomach, kick her in the shin – she doubles over in pain, she gulps with fear – I have her little white neck in my hands, her arms beat the air pathetically, I choke her like a chicken, she tries to scream but can't, the vocal cords crushed between my fingers can only make sounds like the creaking of a rusty hinge, you needn't have bothered with the make-up, Mary, your cheeks are redder now than your lips. Her body gives a final spasm, I release her violet throat, Mary slides down to my feet, like dead seaweed on an ebbing tide. I am relieved, I wipe my satisfied cock on her négligé, put the goods away, button up my flies, I am calm. But I have to run to her house, break in like a common thief; Ace is covered with an embroidered sheet, a black ribbon around his neck, his head has doubled in size. Into my pockets I stuff Mary's jewels, cheque book, credit card, purse, the cash stashed in the salt cellar in the kitchen, on the old typewriter in her son's bedroom I write the following letter: 'I like travelling too, darling. Goodbye. Don't bother looking, you won't find me. Mary.' I think this an extremely bad show on her part since poor Peter Bushy spent his life driving enormous rigs as far as Baghdad and Kabul to be able to feed his little family. Finally, I cram her dresses, trousers, a jacket, a blouse and shoes into a suitcase and go back home.

I took a spade, fork, and a pickaxe from the shed and began my work at the foot of the apple trees, which are in bud in May. Three long hours of digging it took me to uncover the cellar wherein repose my first two wives, alongside a mistress and an over-greedy blackmailer who, from a window in

Strangeways, had spotted me burying my second wife. He got out on parole two years early and began paying me visits with the aim of getting rich by making me poorer. He was a small man, thin and shy, who always wore a navy blue suit, a tie, a beige raincoat and a hat when he came to see me. He'd been a bookkeeper in a large printing works, where he'd fiddled a lot of money, which had caused the ruin of several small suppliers and nearly bankrupted his own company. When he knocked at my door I used to watch him for a while from an upstairs window, he looked like he was a bailiff or from the Inland Revenue. He was polite, courteous, he always accepted the cup of tea I offered him as he sat in my dining-cum-living room, sometimes he would even take a drop of something stronger, but he never wanted to be a bother or to take up too much of my time. He had a bony neck and spotty skin, he spoke with the merest movement of his lips, so softly I had to lean forward to hear him.

'Believe me, Mr Blain, I sympathize with your predicament. It's entirely understandable that a man might want to bump off his wife. But you see, the fact that you told the police she'd disappeared means you have no rights to her estate until you can prove she's dead. Also, you really shouldn't have let yourself be seen burying the poor woman in your garden. If you'd avoided that fairly obvious mistake then I wouldn't feel obliged to ask you to pay me an amount corresponding to a decent wage, at least until I find myself a job.'

He dropped by each week for his money, I always expressed interest in his professional life, he always answered, in a voice full of disgust, that he'd applied to such and such a company, that he always left the interviews humiliated, that chronic unemployment was making his social reintegration very difficult. One afternoon, by which time I was certain that he lived alone and had no accomplices, as he sat in my living-cum-dining-room-cum-study before the tea and biscuits, I put a sleeping tablet strong enough to knock out a horse in the teapot and myself drank the little that was necessary to ensure he did not smell a rat. I was a little woozy by the time he conked out on the sofa, and I staggered a little as I laid him out on the floor and pressed a goose feather pillow onto his face. He jolted a few times, then died painlessly. I fell asleep, my head resting on the pillow, and woke a few hours later stretched out over his cold body. That was the end of Albert Exton.

It was an exhausting night, I wasn't as young as I used to be, the earth hadn't been opened to such a depth in four years and it required enormous effort to raise the roof of the cellar, which was made of three sheets of corrugated iron welded together. The cellar's walls were made of concrete, but the floors were earth so that the bodies would decompose as quickly as possible. I built it fifteen years ago, digging down from inside a shed so the neighbours wouldn't see me. I thought I'd only have to use it the once, for my dear Eleonore, a fickle, cruel and authoritarian wife. I put her there six weeks after I'd finished the job, her tongue was black and bloated, her big blue eyes hanging out of her head, her bony fingers looked like they'd been planted in her neck. She loved Irish stew, she had taken a second helping; the poison quickly took effect, after barely three hours of convulsive suffering in my protective arms she left this world of ours. She was small, the cellar seemed far too big for her, perhaps I knew intuitively that I'd be making use of it again, but at the time I believed she would be the chamber's only resident. I demolished the shed that had hid my labours, it was getting in the way of my beloved apple trees and didn't fit in with the rest of the garden.

The night I buried Mary was, in comparison, one of panic and improvisation. There were two very serious alerts. Old Benton, who always takes his dog out on the street before his supper, had let him out into the back garden at a very late hour because Jerry apparently had cystitis and was pissing all over the house. Benton was going to have to put him in the garage for the night. I leant on my spade, he leant on the fence, it was past midnight, I explained how busy I'd been all day and that if I didn't plant the shoots that had been delivered earlier they'd be dead by the weekend. Benton knew as much about gardening as I did about hot air balloons, he nodded wisely, his white moustache danced in front of his indistinct face. I was in a cold sweat for the five minutes he chatted to me before seeing to his fox terrier and his cystitis. An hour and a half later, I'd unearthed the roof of the cellar. I was dripping with sweat, trembling and entirely out of breath, when the neighbour from the other side, no doubt suffering from insomnia, decided to get some fresh air and noisily threw open his bedroom window. I barely had time to jump into the cellar, and as I landed, I could hear the crunching of bones under my feet. I remained hidden for about ten minutes among the remains of Eleonore, Jane, Liz and Albert. I could see the glow of my neighbour's cigarette, his light-coloured pyjamas, I didn't have the strength to wait until he went back to bed, I silently vomited my dinner on top of the now more or less fleshless bodies; I thought of my good old William, I recited in my aching head: 'O God, I could be bounded in a nut shell and count myself a kind of infinite space, were it not that I have bad dreams.'

I was exhausted by this new trial. I dragged myself back to the house and undressed Mary, who really was a fine specimen, even if she had lost her wonderful suppleness now that she'd been dead for five hours. I knocked back two glasses of whisky and swaddled her in her black coat: her milky white skin would be almost phosphorescent in the moonlight. I took her in my arms and carried her out to the pit where I gave her a last kiss on her blue lips before leaving her among my little group of departed souls. I put the roof back, filled in the hole and unrolled the turf like a carpet – out of sight, out of mind, as Mother says. At dawn I went to the Salford dump and there, among the mountains of rubbish, disposed of the clothes and suitcase that had belonged to Mary Bushy, Mary who had gone on a trip, peace be with her. Peter was distraught and inconsolable for three years, their son never finished his electrician's apprenticeship in Birmingham, he became a car thief and is now behind bars in Leeds. So, Peter Bushy, I'll have the last laugh even if you do think it makes you a hard man to throw a poor sixty-year-old out onto the street, where he bashes his head against the tyre of your lorry and twists his neck and ends up lying in a pool of engine oil, even if you do think you're a gigolo with your new lady love, with her sun-bed tan, her punk rock outfits, her cheap jewellery, and her poodle with its ears pierced like Swiss cheese and horrible big rings hanging from them. She can well laugh from her bedroom window, the cigar between her black lips, like an empress watching the agony of some Christian martyr, but, Peter, I can console myself with the knowledge that I made a cuckold and a widower of you. That's what I mutter at him under my breath, my jaw set. I'm angry again, Bushy, you'll pay for this, I'll get my own back on you and your thirty-tonne truck.

I got to my feet, I was dignified, I went home, meeting no one on the way – the truck hid the altercation from the neighbours. Bushy was the only weak link in the market I had created, everywhere else the journalists are going to have to pay to take their photographs. My kitchen was full of the smell of fuel oil, I threw my trousers and underwear into the washing machine and went upstairs to the bathroom to give my buttocks a good rub, I didn't want to smell like an oil tanker when Louise came by that evening for a cup of tea.

· Chapter VI

It was while I was taking a prolonged sitz-bath – into which I'd poured half a bottle of rose water – that I thought again about what Mother had said the night before. I can't let myself be led like a lamb to the slaughter. If the governor of Strangeways won't stand up for his staff, then I'll have to stand up for myself. I wanted to ask Louise how I could get the right to reply on television. She'd agreed to come over for a cup of tea, and as I was still being pursued by the stink of engine oil I'd decided to resort to drastic measures. Louise arrived at around five o'clock, beaming, dressed in blue trousers, a red pullover and white moccasins – I thought for a moment that we should spend the weekend in the country. We drank tea, ate apple pie, we smiled at each other, said nice things and exchanged wooing glances as we played whist, and the question didn't re-enter my mind until the moment when, finally conquered – it was after seven – she threw herself into my arms and whispered:

'Henry, it's incredible! Your skin smells of . . . roses!'

This did make me feel relieved, but I felt it was not the moment to ask her how to exercise one's right to reply on the telly. Her velvet trousers were already enough of a problem. They were very fetching on her, but impossible to remove in a dignified manner. They were skin-tight, and I resented the fact that Louise had put this obstacle in the way of our first frolics. We finally got them off, she seemed a little afraid, judging from the way she exaggerated her arousal when our tongues had ventured only timidly beyond our lips and my hands had only just begun to blindly explore her thighs and her bum. Louise didn't have the dexterity of Mary, who was able to undo my flies without me even noticing. I had to unfasten my belt myself, undo my buttons and wiggle like a snake to get my terylene trousers down around my ankles. I felt Louise's warm and tender thighs against my own, she was wheezing, we were finally naked, at least from the waist down. Louise was getting warmed up, our mouths fused in frenetic kisses, I felt under my caressing fingers her vulva, humid and swollen with a rush of excited blood, my knob pointed up at the sky like the head of some religious fanatic towards his god, suddenly Louise lifted her head – she looked as if she was removing her snorkel after surfacing from a dive into deep waters – opened her eyes wide and, giving me a very serious look, murmured in a lifeless and trembling voice:

'I'm a virgin, Henry . . .'

'Shit! Oh, sorry, Louise, I was just thinking of the flannelette on the sofa and . . .'

Good Lord! The sweet hymen, I think as I run to the kitchen, holding my penis in my left hand so as not to bang it against a chair or a door frame, with my right hand I grab two clean tea towels from the cupboard above the extractor hood. I've never deflowered anyone before, calm down, Henry, be gentle. Even if she's fifty she looks more like forty and it'll be a great experience. My dick is still trying to reach the stars, be calm, Henry, detached, Buddha-like, breathe deeply, we don't want you ejaculating before you get back to the sofa, where Louise patiently awaits you, like a doe waiting for a stag. On tiptoe I return to Capua, oh, my dear virgin, raise up your buttocks, let me slide this cloth under your pure and immaculate body. Louise is obedient, and it is upon a white background with red squares that our bodies again intertwine and our tongues go into action again. The moment is come, I place my dick in her hand, she holds it like the handle of a suitcase, like a hand-rail. That's it, gently does it. It's like trying to manœuvre two space ships, the American and the Russian vessels hooking up out there in orbit, I have a cramp in my right calf, in the leg that rests on the ground to support me, I have a furious desire to suddenly shove myself into the warm depths of her flabbergasted cunt, her cunt that is as yet only half conquered.

'Are you all right, Louise?' I ask. 'OK?'

'I'll be fine,' she responds.

I'm in there, it feels as though my stomach and back are being wrapped in velvet. I go for it, I go for it with little restraint, Louise goes with me, she pulls me, she pushes me, her hands knead my fleshy hips, our breath mingles, little groans of pleasure are born deep within her throat.

'You like that, Louise? Good, isn't it?'

'I can't feel anything, Henry . . . at the start it hurt a bit, but now, nothing! I might as well be reading the paper!'

I ask her why she's been groaning and purring like a cat. She says she's seeking pleasure, she's 'soliciting' it. Her frankness would vex me were I not a mature and compassionate man. Nevertheless, I can not prevent my knob going soft, I lose my rigidity in the face of her indifference. On the checked tea towel there is little more than a light, pinkish stain, her hymen has been very discreet, I think perhaps Louise has spun me a yarn, if she's a virgin I'm the Holy Ghost.

We went back to work several times in the course of the evening, punctuating our embraces with long pauses that were alternately dazed, embarrassed or talkative. Louise tells me of the impotence of her first husband, we discuss impotence among animals, does it exist? Are there impossible or ill-fated couplings among giraffes, for example, or among gazelles? We feel intelligent, we philosophize, I've fetched my dressing gown to cover our naked legs. We eat Stilton on crackers, we drink sherry, I fill glass after glass, we grow ever more supple. Louise learns quickly, each time I pay her a visit she feels a little bit more, it's as though her cunt is coming to life.

'You might say you're breaking me in . . .'

'Maybe, but the pupil can often outshine the master!'

That at least is my secret hope. Louise roars with laughter and our tongues again become entangled in an interminable kiss. This latest attempt really must be the last, I'm exhausted, this is sapping my strength. I think Louise senses this, she works harder than ever, her back, her stomach, her buttocks, her thighs, right down to the heels that stick into me like spurs into an old nag, she adopts a smooth rhythm, slow and regular, she smiles, she trembles, her hands knead my chest.

'Henry! Henry! Henry! Henryyyy! Hen! Riiii!'

There we go! Louise has set foot in heaven, and so have I, it's as though I've disappeared, sucked up by my cock into Louise's warm, tender and firm cunt. She's all excited by her discovery, this new sensation astonishes her, 'it's a blessing,' she says, carried away on a wave of euphoria. Forgive me! She pulls herself together, makes a vague sign of the cross. She swallows a glass of sherry in one go, she wants to go at it again.

'I've been missing out for the past thirty years! Come on, Henry, come on!'

I explain that I'm tired, I need time to regain my strength. She's piqued, she's seriously pissed off, she gets dressed in a hurry, she grumbles, she wants to go home. I beg her to stay, I show her my resting, dangling gear stick.

'I can't do anything about it. It's got a will of its own.'

'There are ointments you can use.'

'Ointments?'

'Aphrodisiac ointments! From Tibet . . . Good night, Henry, sleep well and sweet dreams.'

There is mockery in her voice, I drag a 'maybe' out of her with my 'see you tomorrow', I pursue her to the hall door, my black and white striped dressing gown around my waist. No kiss goodnight, not even a look, no acknowledgement of the carnal pleasures we've just indulged in. The door opens onto the badly lit street, it's drizzling, Louise trots off into the grey night. I jump. Tom and Jack are in the hall a yard behind me, I'd completely forgotten about them. They have difficulty remaining serious, they're itching to make bawdy remarks, their eyes shine with salacious innuendo. My hair is in a mess, my chest is bare, the dressing gown is wrapped around my lower body like an old floorcloth.

'So what about this final assault, then?' I ask, to save face.

'Final assault? Oh, yeah, the final assault! It's off for tonight on account of the rain. But it'll probably be tomorrow. Sparks will fly, I'm telling you. The cops are installing their sound system.'

I've no idea what they're talking about, they're not setting up a disco, are they? I don't dare ask them to explain. I want them to clear off, and quick! I move to one side, we say goodnight, and goodbye.

I polish off the second bottle of sherry as I watch the news. The Strangeways mutiny is once again the top story. I see worn-out old images of people covered in blood being carried out of the prison on the second day of the revolt. The newsreader says they were the twenty or so sexual offenders who had been severely beaten by other prisoners. Now we see the entrance to the accident and emergency unit of a hospital, a doctor in a white coat is being interviewed. One of the injured has died today after further internal haemorrhaging. The doctor, forgetting his oath of secrecy, declares that until now he'd never had to treat a patient who'd been tortured. There is a sharp intake of breath in the news studio.

'There has as yet been no confirmation that prisoners have been hanged in the part of the gaol that is still in the hands of the mutineers,' says the newsreader. 'Meanwhile, there were violent incidents overnight in an institution for young offenders in Leicester, and a prisoner was found burnt to death in his cell after a riot that broke out this morning in Dartmoor prison near Portsmouth.'

They show an overview of the redbrick prison, a plume of black smoke rises into the air. The commentator continues.

'The ringleaders were brought to Bristol prison, which immediately provoked unrest in the jail. Four of the six hundred prisoners seized control of three wings of the building. Seven mutineers were injured during the incident.'

The newsreader speaks in sombre tones, no doubt mimicking the government's anxiety; it's turning into a farce, this mutiny virus that's infecting the whole country. He puts on a worried look that fails to conceal his jubilation.

'The prison revolts, coming as they do after the violent protests against the poll tax and alongside rising inflation and interest rates, have darkened the political climate and appear to have paralysed Mrs Thatcher's government.'

Then he turns to Peter Jenkins, whose political commentary is gaining ever more listeners. Jenkins always wears a fluorescent green bow tie, which might well be the first thing he puts on in the morning when he gets out of bed. It's his trademark, nobody else on TV would dare wear a green bow tie, they'd be accused of plagiarism. He's red-haired, strong as an ox and very popular on account of his being on the national Rugby Union team. Go for it, Peter! He doesn't mince his words, he says the Strangeways affair must be seen as the latest in the string of Third World-type catastrophes that have afflicted our country in recent years. He raises his thumb and cites the fire in King's Cross station, he lifts thumbs and index finger and cites the Clapham rail disaster, he brandishes thumb, index and middle finger and talks about the people trampled to death at the Hillsborough football stadium. There are three factors in each of these disasters, he says, his hand still up in the air, the three fingers level with his face. Too many people massed in archaic facilities run by incompetent staff. At which point I jump to my feet and and shout out: so just who are the incompetent staff? The screws? The superintendent? The cooks? The governor? Hell! Just give me two minutes in your studio!

The newsreader nods unctuously, he's buttering Jenkins up.

'Your analysis does seem to be confirmed by the preliminary findings of the Woolf inquiry. And more recently we have learned of the state of the kitchens and the food served to the prisoners in Strangeways...'

'It's distressing! Animals are given better food.'

Smack! My slippered foot slams into the sofa. I switch off the television and hurl the remote control at the bookcases. I'm getting sick of this. Why don't they open a gourmet restaurant for the bastards? Norton is forever telling me that our pay slips are proof enough that keeping so many people locked up costs a fortune. As for the governor's denial, he knew exactly what he was doing with his comment about lame ducks among the staff! Well I'm not about to let myself be dragged through the mud. Keep my head down! My arse! I'm going to talk to Louise about this. I'm not surprised they want to get this mutiny business over with, it's spreading across the whole country, they're scared shitless. But I'm not!

This morning I went to the supermarket in Preston Street to do my shopping for the week. I filled my trolley with food and drink, I would like Louise to dine with me tonight at my pretty, candlelit table. The sun shining, it's summery like the day I met Mary in the car park. When I get back to my house I find the whole area in turmoil. Next to the chocolate and candy floss stand there is now a fish and chip van with four tables and a couple of chairs under umbrellas in front, there's a burger van – 20 different burgers for 20 different tastes – and a small truck serving pizzas to eat here or take away. Further along I find people selling phosphorescent toys, African and Oriental trinkets, and there's a shooting range with bouncing balls and plaster pipes. The main road has been transformed into a fairground, which comes to an abrupt end sixty yards from the prison when it meets the police line. My estate is swarming with people, many of them people from the posh areas who would normally never deign nor dare to come here. They stroll around with their pink children and their pedigree dogs, they wander among the police vans parked just about everywhere, inside which officers play cards, listen to the radio, or snooze. But there's nothing to see, just a few rooftops with slates missing, on which one can occasionally glimpse the silhouette of a mutineer. Most of the prison buildings remain invisible behind the row of houses and the police barrier. The real show today is here in the street, where there is an almost festive atmosphere, where the people eye each other up as they walk about. I even see some of the rich folk munching greasy, steaming chunks of fried fish or biting into hamburgers oozing with ketchup. Raucous music belts out of the shooting stand, punctuated by the thudding of rifles. I put my shopping bags on the ground in front of the stand, I hit five targets in five shots, I haven't lost my touch. I win a stuffed dog dressed up as a bobby. I spot David O'Connor hanging about with his drunkard wife and the three kids they have that are old enough to take out for a walk, I march up to him, he smiles at me and I hand the police dog over to the eldest boy whose blue eyes suddenly light up.

'Thanks, Mr Henry,' he says slowly.

The mother and father thank me in turn, but the two other boys begin howling, why can't they have a stuffed toy too. Old O'Connor is going to have to fork out for at least two more goes with the guns, but since he's got a squint and doesn't see at all well, he's going to look silly in front of his kids and will probably only win a keyring or worse. He confides, as I prepare to leave them to their family squabble, that only three journalists had come by yesterday and they'd turned on their heels the second he told them how much he wanted.

'You shouldn't be too greedy, David!'

I have to shout at him to be heard above the racket the three brats are making as they fight over the dog. O'Connor's face, usually so calm and pleasant, has clouded over, it's grey, lined with worry, he's mightily upset by his sprogs' fisticuffs. His skeletal wife stares at me with her feverish eyes, eyes stupid with alcohol. I skedaddle, I have to make a big effort not to burst out laughing at the ruckus I've caused with the stuffed toy.

Some of the rubbernecks have brought binoculars and are giving a running commentary on the state of the roof and what the prisoners look like.

'They're so young!' exclaims a middle-aged woman.

'They haven't shaved, and they're dressed in rags,' adds an old man in a camelhair greatcoat and a tartan cap. 'They really do look like convicts!'

'They look like the galley slaves in *Ben Hur*,' chirps an overexcited young woman.

Most of the mutineers, I can count nineteen of them, are sunbathing in their vests or with their chests bare, swallows on a high voltage power line. From time to time they wave at us, some of the strollers respond, usually the women or the children. We raise our heads, the air has suddenly been filled with the throbbing of engines and the whirr of blades as two helicopters appear in the blue sky as if out of nowhere. They fly slowly over the prison, the pilots try to descend to the level of the roofs, but the prisoners have stood up and are throwing bricks and stones. One of them stumbles, he loses his balance, slides down the roof, grabs onto a joist and manages to stop his fall two yards before the gutter and the void. There are cries of terror from the rubbernecks, but the man has got back onto his feet, a little unsteady, there's much whistling and applause, the helicopters move off, the prisoners give cries of victory, the applause from the street grows louder, I hear people shout:

'Don't give up!'

'You're a disgrace, Thatcher, a disgrace!'

'Thatcher, the people's executioner!'

Police reinforcements have come running up to join their colleagues at the cordon, they look edgy, there is a sort of morbid fascination in the air, the street is electrified for a quarter of an hour by this bizarre mixture of circus perform-ance and prison revolt, then the music from the shooting stand starts up again, things calm down, the party goes on. I won't see many customers today, it's going to be a lean weekend. The journalists have gone to the neighbours' houses and the rubbernecks prefer to stay in the street. Fortunately my contract with ITV runs until tonight, but you can feel in the air that the mutiny is coming to an end, it's like a swan song, tomorrow everything will be back to normal. But just in case, I phone Romeo to ask if he's sending anyone else my way. He seems distant, his voice is hesitant, it's the television that's made him suspicious about me.

'Yes, Elizabeth is fine, yes. Charles is fine, yes, thanks, me too, thank God.'

He says, almost reluctantly, that he's put a few plants aside for me, a rhododendron and four azaleas to go in a corner of the garden, near the apple trees, that he reckons is a bit bare.

'You'll have a lovely coral pink effect when they're in flower,' he adds.

I suddenly imagine the Red Sea, through which I've sailed several times – I was an assistant cook at the time. I'm not asking him to rearrange my garden, just to restore it, to find me a prawn plant, some tillandsias and maybe an aenonium. I'll put his ericaceous plants wherever I want, but I thank him anyway and again praise his skills as a gardener. His voice grows a little warmer after that. But he avoids answering when I ask him about sending people round, he says nothing when I tell him how tough my job is in the prison-kitchens, about how ungrateful the authorities have been by using me to satisfy the public's baser instincts. I'm not discouraged, I tell him again that they say all sorts of rubbish on the telly without checking their facts. Romeo is as stubborn as a mule, he keeps saying the world is going to the devil, there's violence everywhere, it spills over like water from a pot of pasta when the gas is turned up too high.

'It looks like God's having a snooze,' I venture.

Silence on the other end of the line.

'Romeo? Hello? You still there?'

'Yeah, yeah, but all this time the devil is working away at his ovens,' he retorts.

I get the message loud and clear, I wish him an enjoyable Sunday and I hang up, I don't know whether he really will help me reconstruct my Arcady but I'm sure he won't be doing any more advertising for the modestly priced show in my back garden. I telephone Suzan Carlos Simson, but get Ulysses, who works in the pub on weekends. I introduce myself, in his mellifluous voice and his Brazilian accent he asks me to hold the line, he'll get Suzan for me, she'll be right there. What a joke! Suzan keeps me holding for nearly five minutes, charming.

'I never knew you were so busy on Sundays,' I say, a little aggressively.

'At this time of day I don't usually answer the phone, Blain.'

I tell her I'm disappointed, I was expecting her visit, I wanted to show her the damage, the carpet of paper flowers, the mutineers on the roof, I was even going to make her a nice lunch, she says she saw everything on the telly, even stuff you wouldn't be able to see from my place, the interior of the prison, the gangways, the cells, the yards, the kitchens: I act dumb, I make as if I haven't picked up on her perfidious insinuations, I tell her she'll have to come by very soon, the show's coming to an end, you'd better tell your customers, it'll all be over soon.

'Blain, I haven't got time for this now, there's customers waiting to be served!'

I change tack. I tell her it's important to witness it with your own eyes, so you can speak about it to future generations.

'You'd think it was the Holocaust to hear you, Blain. And if you're such a militant why don't you organize some sort of operation from your house? You of all people could bear witness to what goes on inside that prison. I've got to go.'

Slam! I feel hatred invading me like blood poisoning. The ignominious rumours about me are being spread like perfume through the air, my followers are deserting me, I'm going to get into that television studio, they're going to listen to me, keep my mouth shut, the governor says, well screw the governor! What they said and what they showed about the state of the kitchens is true. But why do they never mention that bastard Norton? O'Friel's protecting him, that much is clear. And even if I do give the lags stuff that could only very vaguely be called food, at least I do it tastefully, I play on their stomachs and their bowels as though I were giving a concert on the organs of Saint Paul's. More than that, even, it's a symphony orchestra I conduct, I am the maestro of all the arseholes in my closed little community. Thus I feel doubly betrayed by the prison authorities and their media accomplices. Which is why, disregarding the hunger that is tormenting me, I do not hesitate. I run up to the attic. Tom and Jack are playing cards, they're bored, my arrival wakes them up a little, they're still titillated by my scene with Louise in the hallway last night, they greet me with knowing winks.

'She's a bit of all right, your bird,' they confide.

'Yes, but she's a tropical bird, she needs a tropical downpour to get her in the mood,' I reply, to please them.

Jack guffaws, Tom smiles lecherously, I hadn't noticed the lewd look before, from this podgy man who's always immaculately dressed and so composed and silent.

'We're going to get some good pictures tonight, we heard from sources in the Home Office that this time it really is the final assault, they're going to use helicopters, projectors, public address systems, water cannon, grappling irons, stun gas, specially trained officers . . .'

'The whole thing would've been over long ago if they'd sent in the paras,' I say, half-heartedly.

'That's exactly what they were thinking of doing, Henry. Ivor Searle, the vice-president of the prison officers' association, told Waddington that the profession had had enough humiliation, it was time to send in the SAS. But his members refused, they said it'd be like using a sledge-hammer to kill a flea, they looked foolish enough already!'

'Speaking of humiliation,' I quip, 'have you noticed how badly I'm being treated by the television?'

Their jaws drop, their faces are suddenly drawn.

'So this is what I propose,' I continue. 'I want to do another interview by way of reply, I'm going to spill the beans, put everything out on the table, the management's skulduggery, Norton's wheeling and dealing, that'll give Justice Woolf and his inquiry something to chew on. What do you say, lads, it's a scoop I'm handing you on a plate! If I'm going down then I won't be going down alone!'

They look annoyed. Jack stares at his feet, wringing his hands nervously, Tom clears his throat and gropes his tie.

'It wouldn't be bad if we shot it with that lovely sun in the background, don't you think?'

'We'll have to speak to the boss,' Tom croaks.

'You mean your producer, the one I met?'

I stand there and show no sign of leaving. Tom makes a decision.

'We'll call him straight away.'

He rummages in his bag for his mobile.

'I'll wait for you downstairs. I'll open a bottle.'

I march down stairs and phone Louise. She seems quite aggressive, perhaps because our frolics last night were too brief to satisfy the thirst that has awoken in her body. I describe the food I bought for her that morning, the Irish salmon, the prawns fresh from the Pacific, the vegetable terrine, the Stilton, the bottle of vintage Torres, the raspberry sorbet and the champagne. Louise relents, she agrees to come round just like yesterday at five o'clock. I'm happy, I do a little waltz round the room.

As I replace the receiver, I hear my two reporters running down the stairs. As I grab the bottle of Napoleon brandy from the drinks cabinet, they burst into the room.

'It's on. The boss gave us the green light.'

I quickly see that he did more than give them the green light, he encouraged them without hesitation to do the interview, he reckons he's got a scoop, the goods that will break the scandal. We sit down, we clink glasses, Jack confirms that with the sunlight they will indeed get 'some lovely pictures'. Tom explains that to get a fresh perspective they could film from the front of my house, on the gravel path, with Strangeways in the background. I reply that I'll shave and put on a tie. We raise our glasses. Cheers! The sensation of the alcohol in my throat and the knowledge that Louise will be here in three hours gives me strength for the task that lies before me. We discuss the questions that will be put to me, we drain a second glass and I go upstairs to get ready. I return all spruced up, the skin on my cheeks soft and perfumed. Tom thinks I'm a bit stiff, he has an idea, he places an index finger on his temple, it has to be 'intimate, relaxed, realistic', and definitely not 'official, uptight, or aggressive', he thinks my black-striped dressing gown would be 'very photogenic'. I could still wear the tie and the blood-red shirt.

'OK, Tom. OK, you're the expert.'

They put a bit of rouge on my cheekbones, a beige powder on my forehead and nose to absorb the light and prevent reflections. Jack offers me a fat cigar from his metal case, but I'm not used to smoking them. Tom says it'll make me look more cool, I sniff it and nod in agreement. When we go out into the street the place is more crowded than the banks of the Irwell on a fine summer's day. The party's in full swing, two more vans selling beer and giant lollipops are now parked on the corner, as well as a horse-box inside which a man spins a wheel of fortune and calls out the winning numbers through a microphone linked to an enormous speaker fixed to the roof. Kids scream and play at soldiers, chasing each other through the ever thicker crowd, all of Manchester has turned up to watch the last night of the show. Tom and Jack curse the racket that prevents them from testing their sound levels properly. They film the front of my house, freshly painted last spring, with me in profile as I open the front door, the interview is going to take place in my living-cum-dining room, with me sitting comfortably on the sofa, one hand posed on the arm-rest, the bookshelves in the background. I've poured myself another glass of brandy and have lit my cigar, I'm draped in my black stripes. Tom begins by asking me anodyne questions about Manchester, about my family – my answers are brief – my professional life, my workplace, the particular rules that govern it. I smile, suck on my cigar, and raise my glass to my lips, all this pleasantly punctuates the run-up to the revelations, until the moment when he asks me with a wink – this is the signal – if I was offended by what was said on television about the deplorable state of the kitchens and the food served to the inmates of Strangeways.

'Yes, I felt I was being attacked! I am the head cook, after all. It's not me who built the kitchens, who maintains them, who modernized them, who does the books or looks after the stock. All I do is cook! And what they showed was in fact only . . . the tip of the iceberg (I'm pleased with my suggestive expression). I work in ageing facilities which are only properly cleaned once a fortnight. The place is crawling with rats and cockroaches! The gaol was built a century ago to house 600 prisoners and today there're 1,600 in there! The pipes get blocked all the time, they can't handle the amount of waste water that goes through them, the basins are always full of dirty water that takes ages to drain away, they're always filthy. For years I've been asking for a toilet to be built near the kitchens, we have to cross two courtyards to relieve ourselves. We get so busy at times that my assistants prefer to urinate into the sinks or in a corner of the stock rooms, on a sack of rice, for example, particularly in winter. And then there're the ones with a chip on their shoulder or who hate the prisoners and think they need to dispense their personal form of justice and who piss into the pots, mind you, mixed with forty kilos of simmering food, a drop of urine never did anybody any harm. It's not me who recruits them, I don't know where or how the management find them, but they're not what you'd call *la crème de la crème*. I need to have an iron grip to keep the whole show on the road!'

I take a sip of alcohol, I puff on my cigar, I savour the taste on my palate, I'm relaxed.

'As for the food, if you can call it that, the store room is where all the dirty dealings go on. If you look at the orders placed with suppliers and the bills they send the prison, you'll see that a wide range of food, of average quality, comes into the prison. It's OK, it's edible. Tins of concentrated milk, stewed fruit, yoghurts, Gouda, Cheddar, tins of beans, tuna in tomato sauce, mackerel, herrings in oil, corned beef, chicken and turkey breast, tonnes of it! Last year, in the space of two months, dozens of kilos of honey, honey, do you hear, came into the stock room. The inmates never get even a whiff of these products! They're sold on to shops or canteens of big companies. Barely a quarter of the money that comes in from this goes to buy rice, pasta that a dog wouldn't eat, half-rotten potatoes, lentils that are more like pebbles, three-year-old kidney beans, chicken wings, pork fat or reconstituted beef, powdered eggs and all sorts of other rubbish!'

'But what about the weekly menu that's typed up and signed by the management before being posted in the prison?' Tom asks ingenuously.

I finish my second glass of brandy, I let three seconds go by, to create suspense.

'The menu, huh! It exists all right, but it's only put up near the door where visitors to the prison or families in the visiting room can see it. But to get back to the point, where does the money go, eh? Where's the other seventy-five per cent of the cash? Gone with the wind, like this puff of smoke from my cigar! Ask Evans Norton, and ask the governor too, while you're at it. They'll tell you just how expensive it is to run a fine big car or to collect works of art. It's a pity that the store rooms were three-quarters destroyed by one of the fires the mutineers lit. It wasn't by chance they attacked that building on the first day of the riot. But I don't think the invoice or order books were burned, the management offices didn't suffer any damage. The people carrying out the inquiry might find it useful to have a look there. I should add that Norton is well in with the gang leaders, the ones who can order a leg of lamb seasoned with fresh thyme, roast veal with mushrooms, salmon from the Baltic, lobsters flambéd in brandy, and Dom Pérignon to wash it all down. No expense is too great for them. There's one who has tatami mats and a futon in his cell, he's the leader of an Asian gang, they serve him top class sushi and sashimi! He eats with chopsticks inlaid with pearls and gold. It's Norton who deals with the suppliers. There are rooms in Strangeways that are reserved for these lads to eat on their own, off a white tablecloth, with the same crockery the queen uses, with silver cutlery, served by a chap in livery or by young Zairean women in turquoise silk dresses dancing the waikiki, yes, sir, that is the truth! With enough money you can buy anything in prison, except the right to leave. And Evans Norton is a master of providing luxury services, he could open a new Savoy in the middle of Manchester! All I do is cook! All I do is try to perform culinary miracles with my grey split peas, my brown noodles, my translucid potatoes, my green chicken wings, and I get the blame. You'll soon see who's to blame! Justice Woolf should start rolling up his sleeves, he's got a lot of work to do.'

I'm on my feet. I'm boiling hot, my teeth hurt and there's fire in my belly. I undo the knot in my tie and crush the remains of my cigar into the ground with my heel. Shit! My carpet! I see Tom making signs at me to sit down, cool, Henry, be cool. I sit down. I point at the camera, I stare into it, I address the viewer directly.

'The inmates are right to revolt, the authorities don't give a damn about them or about any of us ordinary people either! The mutineers are only seeking their due!'

I clench my fist, I wave it in the air, NO SURRENDER!

Behind the camera Jack gives me the thumbs up. He removes his eye from the viewfinder, looking like a one-eyed man who's just regained sight in his bad eye. He's stunned and elated, he has that huge grin back on his face, he's still moving his thumb up and down frenetically.

'Brilliant, Henry, brilliant. By God, you've got guts, you have. We've got the governor's resignation in the bag, this'll make waves right up to the Home Secretary, won't it, Tom?'

They congratulate me again. Jack hugs me with his muscular arms, Tom clears his throat.

'You know, Henry, about the gang leaders, that's not really new, it's always been like that in any prison in the world. But the rest is pretty serious stuff!'

'I always kept my mouth shut but that didn't mean my eyes were shut too. I see what goes in and what goes out of the prison: the west wing, lane five, door D, right next to the kitchens. And do you think they grease the staff's palms, you think we get something out of it? Not a chance. The only thing Norton and O'Friel put our way is the piddling amount we make from selling offal. You see, in my team – it's a legal obligation, written in the rules of the prison – there's a qualified butcher. Unfortunately, very little meat arrives in the prison, and what does find its way there doesn't usually have the required veterinary certificates. Whenever it does it goes straight to cold storage somewhere to be sold on, as I've already said. But we do buy offal which we make into minced meat or spicy sausages. If we can get fifteen tonnes a year out of the offal that's completely unuseable and flog it to dog and cat food factories, then we're laughing! We each of us get about the equivalent of a month's salary. It's a little bonus, if you like, it's not a fortune.'

'What do you mean when you say, "offal that's completely unuseable"?'

'It really stinks! It's disgusting. It must have been what the TV reporters came across after the west wings were stormed.'

I soak a ball of cotton wool in rose water and remove any make-up in front of the Venetian mirror in the living room. Tom and Jack nod pensively.

'It's ... it's a pity, Henry, that you didn't mention that in the interview ...'

'Are you mad, lads? It's not me who's the enemy, I'm only a pawn!'

Another dose of rose water on the face, then I serve a fresh round of brandy while Jack puts away the lighting equipment. Cheers! Dring! there's someone at the door, I go to open it. It's Louise, smiling, half an hour early, in a delightful Prince of Wales check suit that I glimpse under her raincoat, with black stockings and high heels. She's carrying a plastic bag which she hands me.

'It's an apple pie I made, it's still warm, that's why I came a little early ... is this a bad time? You're in your dressing gown, were you having a little nap?'

'No, not at all, it was part of my performance. I'll explain later. Have you seen the crowds of people in the sun? It's like a huge party out there, and all thanks to the mutineers.'

We go inside. The two reporters still have their glasses in their hands, they recognize Louise and greet her enthusiastically. I do the introductions.

'We're all in the same business, whether it's the press or the television,' coos Jack, who keeps winking at me.

I don't reply. I don't look at him, which is why he keeps doing it, he's getting on my nerves. We clink our glasses in honour of Louise. Tom and Jack linger, they're suddenly interested in the *Anglican Tribune*, they ask questions about it, they want to know everything about a paper they'd never heard of five minutes ago. Louise is flattered, voluble, she replies eagerly, her paper is her cause. She talks about its

109

history, about the staff, she describes the different sections, Tom and Jack pretend to listen attentively. Jack slowly looks her up and down, Tom's eyes delve stubbornly into her blouse, seeking out the hollow of her bra and the beginnings of her breasts. Their masquerade annoys me, I clear my throat.

'Don't you think you should be getting ready to film the final assault? Your producer won't be very happy if you miss the start.'

They look at me, get the message, and wish us a pleasant evening, complimenting me in low voices before disappearing up the stairs. I shut the door that opens onto the hall. Louise is irritated by my intervention.

'But they were so nice!'

'The delicious apple pie you kindly brought is getting cold and I have no desire to share it with that pair.'

'Good Heavens, Henry! Are you that fond of cakes?'

I go into the kitchen, unwrap the pie, get plates and spoons from the cupboard. I switch on the kettle, make the tea and think about my interview. I wonder if I wasn't too direct. The way I backed the mutineers was perhaps a little too extreme. My accusations against Norton are well-founded, the proof of his corruption is everywhere, but with the governor it's more of an intuition. Norton couldn't be doing his business on his own, he must be getting help from higher up. It's far from certain that the inquiry will ever go as high as Sir Brendan O'Friel. But at least I feel relieved, I've done my duty – Mother will be proud of me, I'll be rehabilitated with my friends – as for the rest, I'll just have to wait and see.

I don't hear Louise approach. I'm facing the wall by the draining board, putting tea into the pot, the water is simmering in the kettle, I feel her hands on my hips. She presses her body against my back.

'Dreaming about me, Henry? No need to, I'm right here,' she whispers.

I turn my head towards her and my lips fall onto her mouth, which swallows me up, sucks me in, licks me, nibbles. Louise covers me with kisses, a shiver runs up and down my neck, I put the teapot down on the draining board, I want to grope for the kettle, switch the bloody thing off without leaving Louise's lips. I feel her hands sliding gently over my stomach and under my belt, moving slowly, but with precision and determination, towards my crotch, the kettle plug is on the other side of the sink, I can't reach it without disengaging myself from Louise. The water is now gurgling wildly, I should've bought an automatic kettle years ago. My knob suddenly stiffens at the touch of Louise's inquisitive hands, it's as hard as the safety rail on a sixth floor window. Louise is already taking the initiative, she's aware of the effect her kisses are having on my anatomy, her right hand comes out again pretty quickly, she attacks the buckle on my belt and then my flies, the kettle is making a frighening noise, we're in a sauna, bathed in clouds of tropical humidity. I turn to face Louise at the moment when my trousers, the zip now open, fall like a stone to my ankles. I slip my arm around her waist and draw her towards the other side of the sink without ever abandoning her lips, with my free hand I find the plug, pull it out by giving the cord a sharp tug, bastard kettle! A jet of steam burns the inside of my wrist. The gurgling stops, I hear Louise panting, her eyes are closed, her glasses are steamed up, it's so hot in here. It's my turn now to caress her legs, to pull up her skirt, nice material, soft, she's wearing stockings like last Thursday. I feel a strip of skin at the top of her thighs, ah, Louise! What a lovely present, what a metamorphosis after yesterday's trousers that were sewn onto your skin. I feel my dick trembling in the hollow of your hand, crimson with impatience. We draw inexorably closer to the table, Louise's bun comes undone, her grey hair falls slowly down over her shoulders.

'You were dreaming about me, weren't you, Henry?' she whispers.

'We were naked, Louise, like Adam and Eve, we were rolling around on a blanket of white fur . . .'

Crash! A dessert bowl explodes on the tiles, Louise's ass comes to rest on the Formica, the crockery is in for a hard time. I grab her wrist, she was about to place her hands on the table behind her, it would have landed on the apple pie, and made a mark like something from a cave drawing. We laugh at the mess we're making, my hands get inside her green silk knickers, my fingers grab hold of them, I pull gently, Louise lifts one buttock then the other, I get no further, they remain stuck at the top of her thighs, I took a look. Jesus! I forgot about her suspender belt. Good God almighty, it's not the first time she's worn this gear, she could've been a bit more thoughtful, particularly if she wanted to take me by surprise like that, standing up in the kitchen. Louise senses something is wrong, my prick goes soft in her hand, she opens her doe eyes, which I can barely make out through her steamed-up glasses.

'What's wrong, Henry?'

'Nothing, Louise, nothing, you just need to unhitch your stockings, I can't manage it, your knickers are caught . . .'

'I'm sorry, I wasn't really paying attention when I got dressed, and I'm not used to these contraptions, I just wanted to please you.'

'It's all right, Louise, it's all right. But you might need to use your lovely little hands to get my rudder back on course.'

Louise smiles, says I'm a poet. Her fingers tremble, she has difficulty undoing her stockings, her lips begin devouring me again, her stockings slide down over her thighs, which have lost their smoothness and upon which I now see cellulite, I try to overlook this, and abandon myself to her ardent kisses. Louise draws me into the depths of her cunt, my knob vibrates with joy, I feel her heels sticking into my back.

'We're getting there, Henry, we're getting there!'

'Where?' I ask, ever ready with a gaffe.

'Sssh! Don't stop!'

I put the apple pie in the oven to heat up, picked up the broken crockery, and set the table. Water simmered in the kettle, it looked like a brawl had taken place in the kitchen. Louise was talented despite her late start, she reminded me of Mary and even more of Jane, who had been a young nymphomaniac with a disturbing imagination. Perhaps she'd been taking me in ever since our first meeting, I mused as I poured the water into the teapot. The pot overflowed, I was distracted. Louise waited for me in the living room-cum-study, she leafed through an 1867 edition of *Antony and Cleopatra*, a quarto edition bound in red leather, she shouted every other minute.

'I'm hungry, Henry, hurry up!'

I opened the window that gives onto the street, night is there, lit by multicoloured lights, there were just as many people in the street as before, waiting for the show to begin, the music from the fairground vans could be heard even this far away. I closed the window again, drew the double curtains, put the teapot, pie, plates and cups on a tray, and went boldly into the living room.

'It's ready, my dearest Louise.'

She was so affectionate, warm and willing that she had hardly given me time to cook. Luckily I'd planned dishes that needed little preparation. Only the prawns had to be thrown into the pan to be flambéed with raki. The salmon and the vegetable terrine could go straight onto the plates. We dined by candlelight, on a lovely embroidered tablecloth mother had given me for my second marriage. Louise marvelled as she tasted each different thing. She spontaneously thanked God for all the lovely food she had before her, I reminded her it wasn't God who had prepared the meal.

'Don't be silly, Henry, I know very well you're a cordon bleu cook,' she retorted.

We talked about the mutiny. I told her that the accusations made on the television had turned my friends against me, that the two ITV reporters had let me exercise my right to reply, I wanted to be rehabilitated. Louise was moved, she felt sorry for me and offered to do an interview with me for her paper. I had to 'drive the point home', especially now that the mutineers had become so popular. Our conversation was disjointed; often, between two mouthfuls, Louise would leap up and descend on me like a furious hornet, stopping short just in front of my face, which she would then proceed to kiss with such skilful slowness that I could not resist, me who never liked doing two things at once. She even managed to make me fall out of my chair as we were about to start on the Stilton, so expertly did she get my rudder back on course and smother me with perfumed kisses that I surrendered to her on the carpet. We finished our meal in front of the telly, which I switched on for the nine o'clock news on BBC1. During the fifteen minutes of national and international news, the presenter didn't say a word about Strangeways, no sign that the final assault was due to take place this evening, she merely mentioned that the revolt had spread to Brixton and Pentonville prisons in London, and to Stoke Heath, Hall, Cardiff, Armley, Shepton Mallet and Gartree jails. As each name was pronounced they showed a photograph of the place, as if it were a slide show, then the presenter turned to Peter Jenkins, once again the special guest, with his fluorescent bow tie. He immediately diagnosed 'an explosive situation, that could well lead to widespread social unrest.'

'By dint of repeating "more freedom and less state", funding for the prison service has shrunk dramatically,' he went on. 'At the same time there are ever louder calls for more respect for law and order, judges are handing out ever longer gaol sentences and are applying preventive detention, a phenomenon which goes against British legal tradition.'

Then he took a pointer, turned towards a chart and showed, his arm outstretched, that Britain had the highest proportion of prisoners among all the western European countries, it had 97.4 prisoners per 100,000 inhabitants, against Turkey's 95.6. Germany's 84.9, France's 81.1, Italy's 60.4, and Ireland's 55. To end the interview on a lighter note, the presenter asked him how he had got on in the Rugby Union semi-final against Wales that afternoon in Shrewsbury. He smiled and replied modestly that he'd scored three tries. Thomas Hush had transformed them, his team had won by thirteen points, he'd pulled a muscle in his shoulder, because he wasn't so young any more ... I thought he was very seductive, lively, clear, concise, pertinent, he convinced me, I even shouted 'Go on, Peter!' before he disappeared from the screen. It was time to move on to the problems of ground water pollution caused by pig slurry in the Netherlands. Finally, the sports news came on. Football, rugby and golf took up more than half the programme. I liked football, Louise liked golf, we listened for the results. I wanted to see how Liverpool had done, I've always been a Liverpool man, their bad reputation is due to their supporters, the two should obviously not be confused, the players are excellent, and the captain, Dean Holdsworth, is unmatched as a dribbler and as a strategist. Louise was crestfallen to learn that Matthew Mandibaum, a golfer she 'fancied the pants off' because he was so handsome and refined, had not only lost at Saint Andrews but had come third!

My digestion is not too good and I dozed off in front of a

programme called *Out of This World* in which Esther Rantzen and Chris Searle explored paranormal phenomena. They were presenting the case of a certain Jim B. who had been cured of colon cancer by sending a lock of hair and a colour picture taken in a photo booth to a Scottish healer from Guirloch who preferred to remain anonymous. While I snoozed Louise cleared the table, washed the dishes and did her face in the bathroom. Then she uncorked the champagne an inch from my ear, the cork took out a bulb on the chandelier before bouncing off a copper bowl hanging on the wall. An initial explosion, a second one with a white flash and a shower of glass on our heads, then the boom of a gong. I woke up choking, shouting:

'Charge! Charge! Charge!'

It was nearly eleven o'clock by the time we finished the bottle. I made the mistake of telling Louise that the champagne and my little nap had perked me up. She came and pressed herself against me, her lips on my ear, her tongue darting around its hollows. 'Is that right, Henry? Here, can you feel? I've sorted it out,' and she guided my hand under her skirt, her knickers slid effortlessly to her ankles, she quickly pulled them off, her mons Veneris looked like a jewel set in white skin striped with black lace. She'd dimmed the chandelier, the room was filled with soft light, she definitely did have the ability to reawaken my knob, which stood up like the Union Jack flagstaff on the turret of the aircraft carrier *Victoria Queen* on its way to the Falklands war. We didn't bother to undress, it's more aesthetic to keep your clothes on at our age. But her hands stroked my hips, they kneaded my neck, they tousled my hair, I felt her breasts heaving beneath the open top of her blouse, her bun came undone again, her head shook no with the energy of a she-devil, her thick glasses fell off her nose and were lost between the cushions of the sofa, her face was ablaze, there was a hint of defiance in her smile, her hips moved frenetically, her thighs gripped me like a pair of pincers then suddenly opened to precipitate me deep into her lovely warm cunt, ah, Louise! I want my dick to warm your spine, vertebra after vertebra, right up to the halo on your holy head, ah, Louise! We're being carried aloft on a wave of youthfulness, ah, Louise.

But music rends the air like an explosion, an invisible truncheon blow to the head, we can no longer hear our panting, our murmurs of ecstasy, the music bores into our heads, and then an incandescent light, a blinding wave submerges the room, our white-washed bodies become transparent, immaterial, latex sheaths, drained corpses, frozen skins, we will not be going to heaven, Louise. I go soft immediately, this is war, my shrunken prick is like an old radish forgotten at the back of the fridge, it looks like it did when I had fever. My temperature was over a hundred and I felt like a eunuch when I stood in front of the mirror. We are petrified.

'The *Walküre*!' she screeches, her lovely green eyes staring out of the window, 'The Walkyrie!'

'What?' I shout.

'The Walkyrie, can't you hear it?'

'Can't hear you, can't hear you ... are you taking the piss, Louise?' I scream. I feel the floor and the walls shake, my china rattles on the shelves, the earth is about to open up, it's the Last Judgement. Louise is on her feet, she's pulled down her skirt, buttoned her blouse, put on her jacket. She runs to the french windows, opens them, runs into the garden, I can just about make out her silhouette on the terrace. Nothing is real any more, we're being diluted like sugar in a vapour of steely blue light, there are no longer any acacias, hazel trees, no more bower, there is no longer a wall nor roofs nor sky, we are disappearing at the speed of light to the music of the Walkyrie, says Louise with much self-assurance, I believe her. Never in my long life have I seen so many projectors and speakers, they're installed on the towers of Strangeways, like a battery of anti-aircraft guns pointing at the earth instead of the sky in their hunt for underground enemies, the 150mm guns are going to fire at the rats and the fieldmice! I see a helicopter flying over the south wings of the prison, almost above us in the din of the music, it hovers in the air, silent as a kite. The mutineers move around the rooftops, like butterflies in the night, fragile, they run from one chimney pot to the next, they take bolts out of their pockets and aim at the too distant projectors, some throw slates like frisbees, they smash into the side of the helicopter or are sliced by its blades.

'What wonderful music! You recognize it now, don't you?' Louise shouts into my ear.

'No, I don't!'

'It's Wagner. The Walkyrie. Hey, look! There, there! The police are climbing up the walls like spiders. It's all quite spectacular, don't you think, with the music and the light?'

My eardrums are like sausage meat, I can't hear anything any more, it's like the Apocalypse.

'They're trying to unnerve the mutineers, to make them crack, make them surrender. They have to bring an end to all this, after all. So they might as well play Wagner if they feel like it.'

Louise shrugs, she looks a tad contemptuous, like she did the other night in the restaurant. I don't give a shit, I like Beethoven, Chopin and the swing of our American allies. Everything must be brought under control again! To end up unemployed with just two years to go before retirement. It is indeed the final assault, I'm going to get that video cassette back from Tom and Jack and tell them I've no comment to make, everything is just fine now. I'm standing behind Louise, pressed against her back, I wrap my still vigorous arms around her, I kiss her neck and shoulders. She's annoyed, she wants to concentrate on the show. I calm down, we look up into the sky, we watch the revolt being crushed. To judge by the technology and manpower being deployed here, we can safely say that this is still a rich and powerful country.

But we're suddenly pushed aside. Jack wants to get out into the garden with his big camera on his shoulder, we're in his way, he's hysterical, he shouts: 'Gotta get this, gotta get this!' He films, he films, it looks like his head has disappeared inside the camera, he stops in the middle of the lawn, moves to the left, moves back to the right, he walks backwards on tiptoe, he almost falls over but keeps on filming. He's dazzled by the spectacle, he thinks he's the director, he shouts: 'Brilliant! Brilliant!' He does a panning shot, he films the white light, he's making a film of the end of the world. He removes his head from the eyepiece, he's hallucinating, he smiles blissfully at us. 'Incredible, incredible, just incredible!'

Chapter VII

The final assault was a balls-up. Three police officers were seriously injured and seven diehards have continued to defy the British government for the past week. Seven heroes, seven martyrs are still in control of one of the roofs and two of the five floors of Block D in the south wing. Nets were lowered over the building and over the lane that separates my garden from the prison wall. These were not finely meshed nets like the ones I'd asked Romeo for to protect my garden. They were as coarse as goalpost nets, they were to prevent the mutineers throwing themselves to their death in front of the cameras, that would make a bad impression. There was a fortnight of endless negotiations to persuade the remaining mutineers to give up, but they knew it'd be a mistake to do so. They had a very active support group, they were marching towards glory, they listened to the radio, they watched TV, they knew well that there'd been no news whatsoever of the eighteen fellow mutineers who had given themselves up, there'd been no statement about the state of their health nor details of which gaols they'd been sent to. Top secret! Mum's the word! Disappeared! They knew them by name and surname, they recognized them on the screen:

'Look, it's Nym Murray! And that's Glyn MacMorris. Look

at Jason Lawrence in disguise again! And there's George Scroop acting the fool as ever.'

Two days after the show, Tuesday the tenth of April, the prison staff, those who worked in the kitchens, in the library, in the workshops, who did the cleaning, got an official letter informing us that we were technically unemployed until further notice. We should present this letter to the local job centre, who would then pay us 40 per cent of our salary; the prison would generously pay us a further 10 per cent, we would thus lose half our income! One of the caretakers, the chap who looks after the canteen, the showers, the toilets, the walkways, was apoplectic, he wanted to know how he was going to manage to feed his three kids, what with his wife having just been made redundant, and he had a mortgage to pay off, as well as the loans for his car, his caravan and the new kitchen he'd just had installed. I was on the way back from the bank, reading the paper as I walked, when he zoomed into my street in his Toyota. He slammed on the brakes like the cops do on the telly, the car came to a screeching halt that left it sitting at an angle in the middle of the street. His upper body emerged through the sunroof, he was standing on the seat, like a tank commander in his turret, he'd already shouldered his pump gun, he was hurling abuse at the mutineers, screaming that he'd have them. He emptied his magazine twice, eight cartridges in the direction of the prison roof, and hit one of the prisoners in the arm before being surrounded by plain-clothes policemen who carted him off first to the police station and then to the psychiatric hospital, where he remained under observation for forty-eight hours before being handed back to his family, stuffed with tranquillizers. If they hadn't released him we, his colleagues, would've got up a petition for the liberation of Ange Krawscycz, the first man to stand up and fight for our jobs and our pay packets. 'I will not be another victim of these convicts!' he was shouting as they hauled him off to the police station. He may have gone about it the wrong way, and the target he chose may not have been the right one, but no matter! We all chipped in to buy flowers to send to his wife to show that we supported her in her time of trouble. The letter about technical unemployment had nevertheless convinced me that there would be no further attempt at a final assault. The Home Office would henceforth patiently await a negotiated solution with the seven remaining prisoners.

The great Sunday show had come to an end in the middle of the night. I thought I was both deaf and blind when they finally switched off the sound system and the projectors, I thought I would never again hear a bird sing or the wind rustle through the tree tops. Our eyes were burning, our ears buzzed, we were quite groggy. Tom and Jack put away their equipment. According to the terms of our contract they should've left the attic on Sunday evening at midnight, I'd been magnanimous, we'd all been carried away by the night's adventure. I asked them to give me the video cassette containing the interview, they said they'd send me a copy.

'I have nothing to say now,' I explained. 'Everything has gone back to normal, all that should be forgotten, life goes on . . .'

Their attitude suddenly changed, they became sullen. Tom cleared his throat.

'It's already gone to the editing suite,' he grunted. 'We phoned the studio and they sent a courier, around seven o'clock. But we can cancel the broadcast if you want, Henry . . .'

'I'd prefer it if you did, lads, there's no point any more.'

'OK, Henry, OK, it's up to you. But it's four in the morning, so it'll be locked up in the studio now. We'll find the original and send it to you tomorrow. And that'll be that, no problem.'

Off they slunk with their equipment. A taxi was waiting for them outside, I stood on the doorstep to watch them go.

'Bye, Henry, and thanks again!'

'See you, lads, keep up the good work!'

I received the cassette two days later, I placed it on a shelf. I don't own a video recorder.

The last seven mutineers became stars within a few days. Block C had been recaptured during the supposedly final assault and from it cameras were now able to zoom in on the rebels. Which meant that no more rubbernecks or journalists would be paying to watch events chez moi. No one would be interested in the view from my place, things would be much clearer on the TV screen. It was true, the mutineers looked so close on the screen you felt you could almost touch them. They'd all been identified thanks to leaks from prison staff, their names and backgrounds were listed on the nine o'clock news on Wednesday the eleventh of April:

Nym Murray: 23, post office worker. Sentenced to eight months for stealing a bicycle.

Paul Gordon: 30, sales assistant in a Levi's shop. Three years for theft and receiving goods stolen from his company's warehouse.

Glyn MacMorris: 28, unemployed. Sixteen months for a second offence of pickpocketing.

Fred Fluehler: 44, mechanic in the merchant navy. Twenty-five years for a crime of passion.

Dipack Kapoor: 36, unemployed Indian immigrant. Eight years for drug dealing.

George Scroop: 47, former boxer, doorman. Ten years for bank robbery.

Jason Lawrence: 20, pizza delivery man. Two years for selling marijuana.

A photofit picture of each was shown along with footage of them walking on the roof of Strangeways. All the shots were high-angle because the cameras were filming from Block C.

ITV had the brilliant idea on Friday evening – when TV ratings were often at their highest – of inviting the families of three of the mutineers to appear live on an hour-and-a-half long programme. The families were Nym's, Glyn's and Jason's. The presenter explained that the choice resulted from the fact that the incarcerated members of these families were quite young and their kin might therefore still feel responsible for them, and from the fact that two of them were from Manchester, the third from Liverpool, which meant the families did not have far to travel to be on the show. We'd now like to thank them for being here and let's give them a big hand! Thunderous clapping from the five hundred people in the new theatre in Rochdale Road in east Manchester. I was nicely settled on the sofa with Louise, wrapped in my lovely, stripey dressing gown. We were munching tortillas dipped in guacamole, and drinking Mexican beer, it was Louise's idea, she'd brought everything, tonight I was discovering exotic new foods, Louise was glued to my side, her head on my shoulder, she would frequently take my head in her hand and devour my mouth; I didn't want to miss any of the programme, her brusque arousals and her kisses were getting on my wick. Slow and solemn music played as the families arrived on the set. Nym's mother and the parents of both Jason and Glyn marched in hand in hand as though they were about to do the conga, the presenter feigned astonishment.

'It's to show our solidarity!' Jason's father declared in a trembling voice.

Amidst a tempest of applause, they each took their place in deep fuchsia armchairs. It'd all been very well planned, the others on the set included a prison education worker, a psychologist, a Home Office official and Peter Jenkins, the evening's surprise guest. There was a huge screen in the background on which family photos were projected, the parents began to talk about them as though they were going through the family photo album on a Sunday afternoon. For three quarters of an hour we were treated to pictures of Nym, Jason and Glyn, infants in a pram, in a Moses basket, in pyjamas, apple green pyjamas, turquoise pyjamas, pyjamas with ruffles, one in a park near a lake full of swans, one in a bedroom with wallpaper covered in skiers and mountain chalets. Nym had a tricycle when he was a boy, Jason a little car with pedals, Glyn a scooter. The psychologist was quick to point out that the tricycle was perhaps a clue to Nym's later theft of a bicycle, Mrs Murray burst into tears, the presenter asked her what she thought of that suggestion, she had no thoughts at all on it. She showed other images of Nym as a child, next to a Christmas tree, proudly perched on a bicycle, supporting himself with one hand on his father's shoulder – the poor man was to die just six months later – his big sister sitting at the foot of the tree. Then he was shown in cycling gear after winning a local bike race. He brandished a bouquet of flowers, he kissed her mother on the cheek. At the time he travelled by bus or moped, concluded Mrs Murray, he earned an honest living, she just didn't know what had come over him; the psychologist seemed exultant, he nodded assurance but said no more. For Mr and Mrs MacMorris, both in their fifties, their only son was the brains of the family. They both worked for Shell, and had made many sacrifices so that Glyn could study commercial law. Glyn was shown on a merry-go-round and playing the flute in music school. He couldn't find a job after he finished his studies. For two years he went out every afternoon looking for work and came back in the middle of the night, very often drunk. Then he disappeared, there was no sign of him until, four years later, a police inspector called his parents into his office. Jason's mother and father were much older. Jason was a late child, as they say, the last of eight. The mother was a dressmaker who worked from home, the father a miner who'd been unemployed since the strikes in

1986. They had only two photographs to show. One with Jason in his pedal car, and the other a picture of the entire family posing in front of a slag heap after the wedding of the eldest daughter Cathy. The bride was swathed in a white halo against the mining landscape. Jason was twelve, he was standing at the front of the group, dressed up like a little gentleman, he was doffing his top hat to the photographer, a smile lit up his face. Mrs Lawrence didn't say anything, she nodded her head as her husband spoke. All their sons and daughters had jobs. Jason, the baby, was a hard worker, he delivered pizzas and with half the money he earned paid for drama and circus training classes. Why not, if that's what he wanted. At which Mrs Lawrence sat up and gave her husband an earful, pointing at him and saying that at the start he'd been dead set against it, he'd called little Jason a 'lout and an airhead'. Mr Lawrence admitted his sin, 'you don't choose your vocation, it chooses you', he concluded, addressing parents across the world. He discreetly wiped his eyes with his red handkerchief, he pretended to blow his nose, very moving. In the artistic circles within which his son moved he would sometimes smoke 'hatchish', that was how Mr Lawrence pronounced it, he had a small amount on his person when he was searched, he was unjustly accused of dealing. Mr Lawrence waved his packet of Kent in the air.

'I've got more than one cigarette in my pocket, tobacco's no better! It's a drug just like hatchish! Worse, even! Two years in jail for that. In Strangeways, in the same cell as gangsters!'

Mrs Murray applauded, and so did the audience. When they'd finished she went on:

'Do you realize that my Nym has been thrown in with common convicts merely because he stole a bicycle? It's true!'

The Home Office official looked like he was sitting on a pile of hot potatoes, Peter Jenkins said that the sentence did indeed seem severe, he spoke of a two-speed justice system, similar to the situation in the health and education sectors.

Then began a heated debate between Jenkins, the education worker, the psychologist and the Home Office official, who spoke with passion about equality and respect for the law. One blamed the declining role of the family, another pointed the finger at ever rising levels of violence, a third said it all depended on how you look at life, they were all very convincing in their own way, the parents had fallen silent, the programme was drawing to a close when Sandra Murray spoke up to announce that a support group had been set up for the mutineers; the address and the phone numbers appeared on the screen: HSP (Help Strangeways' Prisoners), Tel: 094 433 649, Fax: 094 433 626. Mrs Murray asked everyone to be generous, they'd have to hire good lawyers for their children, who were now facing fresh sentences of up to ten years! The Home Office official interrupted her to say that the damage to the old Victorian prison was now estimated at a million pounds. The figure was met with whistles from the audience. The presenter called for calm and asked the crowd to show more respect. I would join Jack in saying that the last minutes of the programme were 'incredible'. Images of the different phases of the riot were projected onto the screen at the back of the set, luckily the villainous banner was not legible. But at the end of this summary one could observe as never before the seven remaining mutineers, among whom Nym, Glyn and Jason were easily recognizable as the camera in Block C followed them step by step. Their faces, their expressions, even the movement of their lips could be made out. They played ball, they laughed, they fooled around on the roof, it was just like in the family photos, they were seen in the distance, they were like eagles on a lofty crag. Mrs Murray, her hair in a bun, she must be about fifty, badly dressed in trousers and a vaguely beige-coloured pullover, got up from the deep fuchsia sofa where everyone looked like their arse was mired in a barrow of fresh cement, and moved like a sleepwalker towards the giant screen; the images were four times her size, her eyes were fixed on the heights of Strangeways, her hands were held out towards the screen, joined in prayer, as she harangued her son.

'Come down, Nym! Be reasonable! Come down from there! You've made your point, now you must be an example to the others. We'll fight for you, Nym. Please come down, your mother's begging you!'

Nobody moved on the set, the audience didn't make a sound, I was crying my eyes out, Louise took me in her arms without a word.

'Come down, Nym! Do you hear me? Come down!'

That was it. The credits rolled, the presenter got to his feet, overexcited, red-violet-mauve, he just had time to say the ITV switchboard was being swamped with calls before the network segued into Juliet Doris's food programme, *Recipe for Success.* I blew my nose, pulled myself together, knocked back my pint of Mexican beer.

'I'm going to interview Mrs Murray and write a piece on the support group,' declared Louise.

I went out into the garden to get some air, it was raining, the contours of the prison were dissolving into the misty night.

I became an active member of the support group. The day after the programme, the tabloid press went big on Nym's mother beseeching her son to come down from the prison roof. Nym, Glyn and Jason became stars. Meanwhile, Justice Woolf published the preliminary findings of his inquiry. For the moment the prison authorities were accused only of negligence, but it was emphasized that conditions in the gaol had produced a situation that was highly likely to lead to a mutiny, and it was now necessary to examine more fully the role of the authorities in the affair. The mutineers, who'd seen

the television programme, hung out a new banner: WE ALL
LOVE YOU, MAM MURRAY! YOUR SON, NYM. The revolt
continued to spread to other gaols across England and
Scotland. Trouble was most definitely brewing for the top men
in Strangeways, and it was no doubt for all these reasons that
those bastards at ITV decided to take liberties. It was Saturday
the fourteenth. I had a sore throat, my blood pressure was low,
my eyes looked as though they were about to pop out of my
head, my brain felt like it'd been put through a liquidizer. The
doctor had been to see me, he had told me not to go out. I
downed numerous hot toddies, I was in my pyjamas and my
dressing gown, stretched out on the sofa, I was looking more
at the ceiling – it needed a good cleaning – than at the telly,
which droned confusedly in my ears. I suddenly realized it was
me talking on the set. I sat up, I saw myself on the television as
though in a mirror, with the same black-striped dressing
gown, but tonight I was in no shape to be smoking a fat cigar.
I looked like a Greek shipowner sprawling on his aniseed green
sofa, shirt-tie-grey-hair-impeccably-groomed. I looked rich, I
sucked on my cigar, serene in my cloud of smoke, I ranted on
about the horrors of the prison administration, about Evans
Norton's fiddles, I hinted that O'Friel was in on it too, I looked
so dodgy myself that it might very easily be suspected that I
too was pocketing some of the money that came from selling
off the stocks. I'd missed the beginning of the interview, I
didn't know how they'd introduced me. Each and every one of
my words was deafening to me, as though amplified in the
echo of a tunnel, in the nave of a cathedral or in the House of
Lords. I was horrified, Tom and Jack had betrayed me,
millions of television viewers were listening to me against my
will on the ten o'clock news! The reservations, the nuances, the
doubts I'd expressed during our conversation, all had been
edited out, it was forthright, clear cut, everything was out on
the table, like the verdict at the end of a trial. Then I began to

have nervous tics, I blinked, I threw my head back, I pulled on my cigar like a cowboy on his Marlboro, I was speaking more quickly now, thrusting my chest forward, my voice got louder, I was almost on my feet, I threw my cigar to the ground – what an idiot I am, there's a big yellowish stain on the wool carpet – I clenched my fist, I waved it in the air, I shouted: 'The inmates are right to revolt! No surrender!' I was really worked up, I was rallying the troops of Che and Castro, this was a call for resistance, I was the leader. The whole thing lasted at most five minutes, five minutes is a long time on the telly. They'd portrayed it as something exceptional. Something that would set the cat among the pigeons, dynamite. It was left to Peter Jenkins to comment on these extraordinary images, I could feel his embarrassment, I hoped that he would at least be able to praise my courage and my frankness.

'Go on, Peter! Cheer up!'

Peter began every sentence with the words: 'If these statements prove to be true . . .', to which the presenter would invariably respond that it couldn't be a hoax, the person interviewed was none other than the head cook of Strangeways. To avoid repetition. Peter's opening sentence later became: 'If this individual is speaking the truth . . .' At this point, despite my fever, I leapt to my feet, and wham! slammed my foot into the sofa.

'You'd better believe it's true, Peter! I don't take risks like that for nothing. Just invite me on to your programme and you'll see.'

I felt dizzy, blood was throbbing in my temples, I sat down again, trembling. Peter was going on about rampant corruption among senior officials, who were prepared to sell anything: human organs, adulterated medicine, nuclear waste. The trade in food stocks was a mere trifle, but there was nevertheless no reason to overlook it. If the accusations were confirmed by the Woolf inquiry, lessons would have to be learned. I found him decidedly lukewarm, this rugby chap. He then questioned the motivation of the head cook. Why had he chosen to speak out? and why now?

'It's true that rats will always try to leave a sinking ship. He . . . looks rather a jumpy chap, this Blain. His behaviour at the end of the interview was unusual, to say the least. We might do well to take up a point he himself raised and question the recruitment policies of the prison.'

The ringing of the phone interrupted me, I was about to launch into another tirade, this time I'd have put my foot through the telly. One thing is certain, it's all over between me and Jenkins! I don't ever want to hear his voice again, he's yet another one who has betrayed me, I'll zap him with my remote control if I ever see him again! I picked up the receiver, she says: 'It's me,' as usual, and begins her speech without letting me say hello. Imagine, Mam, you got the number wrong, and you were talking to an undertaker or to Prince Charles, but she doesn't give a damn, she just goes on blindly. She talks to me like a general talks to his army after a battle, I'm on my feet in the living room, stiff as a post, a good soldier standing to attention while the medals are being handed out, I'm too old for this, it's ridiculous, why can't you just leave me alone, Mother! But she's proud of me, as she is of her late husband, I haven't let her down, she concludes. I wasn't able to get more than a couple of words in before she hung up. Her voice has anaesthetised me, I sit down, the phone rings again, I answer it, Louise's voice caresses my eardrums.

'And how is my little patient feeling? You're a real hero now, aren't you? You didn't see the news? You did? He's right, that Peter Jenkins, you were a bit too nervous, not composed enough, it's a pity. You know, I wanted to kiss your lips on the screen, but I just can't bear cigar smoke . . . By the way, I'm meeting Sandra Murray tomorrow in the HSP office. I hope she saw your interview, I'd like to talk to her about it.'

I told her that Mother had also phoned to congratulate me, I felt comforted in spite of the fever that ravaged my body.

'I'll be round to see my patient tomorrow evening,' she added.

We said goodbye after sending each other kisses down the line. I had no desire to talk to anyone else that evening, the phone rang so often that I ended up disconnecting it. I was stretched out on the sofa, my eyes closed, in the silence, I was considering the consequences of my statements, I was scared, there was no going back now. I dragged myself to bed about an hour later, going up the stairs was like climbing the hill of Golgotha, I had to change my pyjamas afterwards, they were soaked in cold sweat, my teeth were chattering, my nerves were frayed.

The night ahead was one of terror. For they all came, all of them, one after the other! This had never happened before. First there was Eleonore, haughty, covered from head to toe in a sooty black powder. Her hair was like strips of leather, her face waxen, when she laughed her milky skin appeared in the wrinkles around her eyes and her cheeks. She was as arrogant as ever, she reached out a hand to me, her varnished nails were inordinately long knives, she said:

'Remember Eleonore when you fall. Your body has not reached the ground yet but it has left its plinth, it is falling, the laws of gravity are stronger than the laws of time. Your flesh and bone will smash onto the ground, think of your spouse before you meet your maker.'

Jane followed in her footsteps, riding bareback on a wild donkey on which she rubbed her crotch, her buttocks trembled, she arched her back, the donkey's schlong was as long as an arm, she said:

'Remember Jane's lively bum, her warm belly, her body that embraced you like a perfumed breath. You're still hard, it's the last time sperm will run down your leg, you're hanging from the end of a rope. Think of Jane, think of her blissful skin, when you meet your maker.'

Little bitch! I wanted to scream, but the sound stuck at the bottom of my throat because Liz was there, standing very straight, feet together, arms hanging by her sides, stark naked, her face in a veil of white gauze. She whispered, her words were indistinct, they came faster and faster, it sounded like she was humming, the veil had turned pink, it was turning red, it was filled with blood that dripped out onto the wooden floor, then there was only a faint gurgling sound. Liz danced a few steps, her feet thumped the ground, the rhythm was slow, vigorous, her arms still hung by her side, her red hair undulated and I noticed splashes of blood all over my walls. She said:

'Think of Liz when your blood dries up in your veins.'

Liz hadn't finished her dance when Mary leaned over me to close my eyes, her white breasts brushed against my thin chest, she had the muzzle of a dog, she licked me with her dribbling tongue, she put her ear on my hollow belly, then she once again had a pretty face with bright eyes:

'I can hear the vermin swarming under your skin, Henry, it sounds like a sheet of paper being crumpled. When you go without God into the animal kingdom, remember your she-wolf, Henry.'

I switched on the bedside lamp, I barked:

'Where are you, Albert? What are you waiting for? Albert Exton! Come out so that I can strangle you again!'

There was no one in the room, just a few red stains on the sheet. In the mirror I saw that my nose was bleeding, my eyes were shining black holes. I left the bedroom lights on for the rest of the night, to stop the ghosts coming back, I didn't want to see them again, it would've killed me.

The fever abates as the day approaches. I stay in bed, I leave the phone off the hook, I drink hot toddies, I fast, I'm going to get well soon, in this day and age you're not old at sixty. I snooze a good part of Sunday, I wake to the sound of voices in the street, one of which is shouting into a loudhailer. I get up slowly, put on my dressing gown and peek through the curtains. There are about twenty of them, they're all looking up at the sky as though watching an air show, except they're really looking over the roofs of the houses towards Strangeways. Hold on a second! I recognize that big woman with the hair sticking out of her blue headscarf, that's Sandra Murray, Nym's mother! I soon spot Mr and Mrs Lawrence and Mr and Mrs MacMorris, and Louise! Louise in the middle of the group, to the right of fat Mrs Murray, who's addressing the mutineers through the loudhailer.

'Come down, Nym! Come down, son. Give yourself up. We'll fight for you. We'll get the best lawyers in the country. Nym, Nym, come down!'

I don't have my usual verve or agility as I climb the stairs to the attic. I'm breathless by the time I reach the skylight, which I open. I see the seven die-hards near a chimney stack, they too have a loudhailer, perhaps given them by the authorities to facilitate negotiations. The huge WE ALL LOVE YOU, MAM MURRAY banner is still spread across the roof. Good Lord! Jason, wearing what looks like a chimney sweep's cap, is doing cartwheels and somersaults across the ridge of the roof, he's a true acrobat. George Scroop, the former boxer now dressed up as Batman – it can only be him – is perched on top of the chimney. He looks like a fairground wrestler, he shows off his biceps, puffs out his chest, he's a bodybuilder. But I can't make out the details of his muscular build, next time I must remember to bring the binoculars from downstairs. Nym shouts through the loudhailer.

'Don't worry, Mam! I'm fine. The show goes on. No surrender! We love you, Mam. You're our mascot!'

Look! The turbaned Indian, Dipack something or other, is doing a tango with the merchant navy mechanic in blue overalls, on the next ridge along from where Jason is doing his acrobatics, it's like a ballet, an American revue, it's fantastic! Well done, lads! Well done! We'll have some more great pictures on the news tonight. I go back to my bedroom, I fix my collar in front of the mirror, I brush my hair, I open the curtains and the window. The air is mild, I lean out, I appear discreetly in their field of vision, they don't notice, so enraptured are they by the rebellious acrobats. Louise is the first to spot me.

'Hello, Henry,' she grins.

The others look my way, now they're all staring at me, they see the same striped dressing gown they saw last night on the telly, it hovers over the group like a dark cloud before they finally recognize me, they applaud.

'Bravo, Mr Blain! We admire your integrity! Let's join forces, Mr Blain!'

At a distance of two hundred yards I see a dozen or so plain clothes cops approaching. Louise points them out to Mrs Murray and the pair of them walk towards my door, followed by the MacMorrises and the Lawrences, and also by a pretty young woman and a well-dressed man, a rather serious-looking chap holding a black briefcase under his arm. The rest of the group take their leave, turning their backs on the police officers, who slow their pace, then stop and do an about turn. Louise is under my window.

'Can we come in, Henry? I'd like to introduce you to . . .'

There are eight of them standing on the gravel of my front garden. I'm still quite weak and very much under the weather but they look at me as if I were the Pope at his window in Saint Peter's Square. My heart is warmed.

'Of course you can, Louise, of course. I'll be right down.'

I work on my dignity as I rush down the stairs. They're in the hall, a panel of admirers, we greet each other respectfully, we congratulate one another, Louise does the introductions, it's hardly worth the effort, we all recognize each other from the television, with the exception of Helen, the graceful thirty-year-old woman, who is none other than Nym's sister, and Robert Montfried, who is one of the support group's three lawyers. I invite them to take a seat in my living room, Louise brings in some chairs from the kitchen and offers to make us all a cup of tea. We accept, we settle down, the atmosphere is friendly. I sit on the sofa, I rest my hand on the left armrest, I have Helen by my side, her perfume smells of berries, I'm happy. Louise says the interview with Sandra went exceptionally well, they were 'on the same wavelength', tomorrow she's going to write a long article about the support group. But as it was Sunday and all the parents and friends were together in the HSP office, they decided that the TV show wasn't enough and they should go and talk directly with their children. They display the loudhailer.

'Now we have to act on the legal front,' interrupts the lawyer.

'There are some very big children among them, some of them nearly fifty,' I remark.

'That's not the problem, we're short of parents,' sighs Mr Lawrence, lighting up a Kent. 'Paul Gordon's are in the south, in Colchester, which isn't exactly near, Fred Fluehler's are dead, George Scroop's are too old, they're dying in a hospice in Bedford, and Kapoor is an immigrant. Which makes it all the more difficult to make them surrender.'

'We have to be careful, Mr Lawrence,' said Montfried. 'With the exception of Paul Gordon, they've all got long sentences and are indefensible. If all their parents were to join us, the support group would be discredited. Don't forget that the legal battle is based on the over-long sentences your children received for relatively minor offences and on the living conditions in the prison.'

Everyone agrees, impressed by the cogency of his argument. Sandra Murray has taken off her headscarf, her mop of brown hair tumbles down, she's unbuttoned her coat, her large body fills a long knitted dress the same noodle soup colour as the one she wore on the telly. She gives me a big smile, she talks loudly with a strong accent, cockney vowels more pronounced than they were in the ITV studio.

'That's why, Mr Blain, we were delighted by your revelations, they'll give the inquiry something to chew on. As soon as I saw you, I said to myself: that bloke's got balls!'

Everyone smiles in embarrassment, I have a minor relapse, blood rushes to my head. Louise goes to the kitchen to make more tea, Helen gives me a confused look, this brings us closer together.

'I think that's going a little too far, Mrs Murray.'

'I'm sorry, Mr Blain, I'm sorry. When we heard that Mrs Baker knew you, we said why don't we call on you and see if you might be interested in joining our struggle for real justice.'

'We are the victims of this abuse of democracy and privilege,' whispers Mrs MacMorris.

They are watching my reaction, they await my response. Helen's hazel eyes gently beseech me, her dreamlike bosom is contained by a skintight little pullover, her woollen mini-skirt rides half-way up her thigh. I look at her slender legs inside their black stockings, I'd like to see her again . . .

'I . . . I'm on the prison staff, you know, I'm not supposed to speak publicly about the gaol, it's a very delicate situation . . .'

'You've got nothing to lose,' the lawyer interjects. 'The statements you made on the television will protect you. If they lift a finger against you they'll be as good as admitting guilt.

They can't touch you. Just think – we've received more than 25,000 letters of support and 3,856 cheques.'

'OK, I accept.'

They congratulate me, praise me, we're all happy, we drink the steaming hot tea Louise makes us, we munch biscuits.

On Monday morning I receive a letter telling me that I am sacked. The management is also going to sue me for breaching confidentiality and for libel. Montfried was right, I have nothing to lose now.

Chapter VIII

A wet dog week. I'm exiled from my prison, I shall never again set foot inside Strangeways, I'm barred. I liked it there, it had been my world for the past fifteen years, even if I did go home every evening, I was like a sailor who goes back on board each morning to hug the devilish winds and sail the subterranean, pitch black seas. I was doing my time there, in my own way, with impunity, I was where I should have been, between dark walls that seeped humidity and solitude. The walls of the cells are scratched with inscriptions, like an ancient book, written and rewritten with nails and bones, not to mention the flesh of fingers or the blood of bruised heads that put some colour on the words of hatred and despair. In the corridor that once was used to house those men sentenced to death, their names can be read in the stone, in small letters, big letters, gothic letters even, a futile gesture, ridiculous, a directory of the hanged. How I loved the walls of the prison, an old skin of grime and sorrow, the smell of disinfectant everywhere, even in the kitchens, disinfectant to disinfect time. I shall never again hear the unremitting drone of voices from the loudspeakers calling prisoners to the infirmary, the governor's office, the visiting room, the workshop, the tinny, electric voices of the screws keeping the lags in line, punctuated by the clanking of doors and bolts, the clanking of wheels on the trolleys that ferry the food trays. Everything clanks here, the law smells of disinfectant, it makes metallic sounds and it speaks through loudspeakers. And I, who was master of thirty ovens, twenty sinks, twelve meet freezers, eighteen assistants, 1,600 stomachs, I who was the malicious joker in the hold of this great, immobile vessel, my reign fizzles out twenty-one months before I'm due to retire because of a few words on the telly. Yes, I lament for my prison, my laboratory, my lost power. Of course, I do still have my garden, where I've always worked with great tenacity towards a beauty that is free and almost wild in nature. And every time a shrub blooms, I have the impression that it is my deceased, who lie there just under the earth, who are flowering. So I shall continue to cultivate my garden, but it will not be my repose nor my salvation, as it was before.

It was on account of some flowers that I decided to get rid of Eleonore. She was sleeping in a deck chair in the July sun, wearing a straw hat with some flowers tucked into its band. I wanted to take a photo of her, and placed a bunch of daisies from the garden in her hands, which were resting on her stomach to match the flowers in her hat. But when I looked through the camera viewfinder I realized you couldn't see the daisies very well, so I added two pots of blue hydrangeas at her feet. I took the photo, but still I wasn't satisfied. I brought about a dozen more pots, containing dahlias, lavender, dwarf roses, and placed them around the deckchair to form a rectangular, multi-level flowerbed. At the very moment I was about to take a lovely picture of Eleonore in the midst of all these flowers, just like Ophelia, she woke up. She saw that she was surrounded by flowers, she saw me contorting myself a couple of yards away to get a good shot, she screamed.

'So that's what you're up to! You want to bury me already! You've got some lovely wreaths for my grave! You're barmy, my dear Henry!'

She leapt to her feet, threw the daisies in my face, kicked the pots aside, breaking two or three of them, then began to hysterically trample the flowers without giving me the time either to press the button on my camera or to stop her destroying my horticultural treasures. The pots were disembowelled, the roots pointed skyward, the flowers were crushed, it was like a battlefield. I was trembling with horror and fury, and I began to think it wouldn't be such a bad idea to bury the woman as quickly as possible, Eleonore, who thought she was the bee's knees because she was chief accountant in Marks & Spencer's. A few months later, my Eleonore, whom I had so admired, inaugurated the pit. She lay there with her tongue sticking out, this woman who had been so fond of elegance. Vanity, vanity . . . I reported her disappearance to the police. I learned that she'd had lovers, they were seriously bothered by the investigation, it was a period of great harmony.

Memories come flooding in now that I am being chased out of my kingdom. It always happens like this, bad news always comes when you're feeling low. Since Monday I've been in a depressive convalescence which seems to have no end. Louise, I might add, is again displaying impatience faced with the langour, the cowardice and the distraction of my weary dick. She reminded me that the thyroid countdown had begun.

'What can I say?' I murmured.

She added that there was not only sex in sexuality, but that my thin hands – hands that were well used to caressing women's bodies, I thought – were much too clumsy to make her forget my shortcomings as a man. I was not pleased, I began to look upon Louise as a stranger. It was Wednesday, late in the evening. As we watched the TV news, we'd celebrated Evans Norton's resignation with a glass of champagne. He would be moved to another institution – he was going to run school canteens in a working class area of London, according to rumours from the staff at Strangeways. I was proud to have dragged down with me this dry arrogant beanpole of a man who had dreamt of being knighted, who had wanted to one day be called Sir Evans Norton, who had humiliated me on more than one occasion in front of my assistants and even in front of the lags who distributed the food trays. He would charge into the kitchen, sniff the pots, pretend to taste the food, and cry: 'Christ! It's inedible! Christ! It's shit! Christ! It's scandalous! I'm going to report you. Blain!' At the same time he'd be forcing me to use stocks of very dubious provenance. I had always wanted to be more generous and more creative in the dishes I prepared, I would've liked to give the prisoners a real treat sometimes, it would've pleased me if the food they put in their mouths had tasted heavenly, if it had made them remember they had a palate. It would have been like a miracle, a gustatory mirage, they would have stuffed themselves and afterwards belched with satisfaction, this would have helped them through the weeks of pig swill, during which they would have waited in desperation, like wolves maddened by hunger, howling at the full moon for the unpredictable return of a Christmas dinner. But instead of this, Norton had limited my powers over the souls of Strangeways. I could play on their stomachs but not on their taste buds.

'To your ruin, Evans! Cheers!'

I raised my glass of champagne towards the television screen, Norton was seen fleeing journalists, taking refuge in his fine house, the butler hastily closing the garden gates behind him.

'He was dispensable, wasn't he, Louise?'

'It won't go any further,' she replied. 'The governor won't be implicated. There were two people who were dispensable, you and Norton, that'll be enough for the inquiry.'

'But I'm not dispensable, Louise! You can't compare me to Norton.'

'Listen, listen! The governor's making a statement.'

We listened. O'Friel was standing, dignified and concerned, in front of the administrative entrance to the prison. He said Mr Norton had decided to withdraw from his position until the inquiry was complete. He was an honourable person, he did not wish to hinder the workings of the law, and he was calmly awaiting the day when he would be able to return to his job.

'The allegations made by the head cook are far-fetched and ridiculous. Mr Blain, who was dismissed for professional misconduct, was undoubtedly upset by the mutiny and by the accusations which the prisoners made against him, accusations which unfortunately have proved to be based on fact. I can only assume that he has ... lost control of himself and is attempting to avoid blame at all costs. I have nothing further to say.'

Splash! I threw my glass of champagne in his face.

'Henry! You're mad! You'll short-circuit the television.'

I wanted to stand up and kick something, but Louise held me back.

'Your blood pressure, Henry! Don't get so het up! Stay calm, Henry, stay calm! Luckily it's only champagne, otherwise the carpet ...'

She takes my hands in hers, she asks me to listen to her, she says Norton will agree to keep his mouth shut in exchange for a very generous pension package but that I'm too honest for that sort of thing. I had spilled the beans on television, I had nothing to exchange or to negotiate, nothing!

'All my friends had turned their backs on me! Mother was reproaching me for not fighting back ... I ... I stood up for a just cause!'

'It doesn't matter. If Norton goes down, he'll go down alone and he'll say you were in on it, that'll be his revenge. And it'll be his word against yours. And your word doesn't carry much weight, I'm afraid.'

Louise looks upset, she cuddles me, she thinks her kisses comfort me. The evening was turning sour, but I held back my bile and didn't respond, we carried on drinking champagne. The evening did indeed turn sour. I'd gone upstairs to get some paper handkerchiefs from the bathroom. Louise had followed me, silent as a cat, to surprise me in the bedroom, to throw me onto the bed, her erect nipples on my chest like a pair of revolvers, her tongue darting daintily between my lips, her hands feeling for my flies, gently cupping my family jewels in her warm and tender palm, which could not fail to resurrect my previously indisposed knob. She hoisted up her skirt, her legs were smooth inside their black stockings, her pussy was already exposed, she led me slowly inside, working my knob with circular movements of the hips that were so adroit that we got to the point with little beating about the bush.

Sometimes she's oh-so-concerned about my my blood pressure, sometimes she completely forgets about it. Twenty minutes later, she wanted us to get back to work. I did my best to please her, I ran my hands over her back, over her thighs, I groped her buttocks, I caressed her labia minora, I titillated her clitoris, but nothing doing! I was getting on her nerves, I was pinching her, I was hurting her with my long fingernails. Then she tried to put some zip back into my pecker, she used her hands, her mouth, her breasts, her bum, but all in vain. She stood up brusquely, she was muttering between her teeth, I thought I heard the word 'prosthesis', I took refuge in my slight deafness and impotent convalescence. She went noisily down the stairs and came back up again three minutes later. She appeared in the doorway in her stockings and her suspender belt, her skirt still up around her waist, in her right hand she waved a tube as though it were the torch of Justice or Salvation.

'Tibetan balm,' she declared in a hoarse voice.

I gave a start and sat up, my back against the headrest, panic-stricken. I asked her if she was sure the stuff was safe, if there was any risk to either of us, you can't smear any old thing on your mucous membranes, Louise! She conceded that it wasn't the sort of thing you can buy in a chemist but she knew the lady in the shop, an ageless old Buddhist with limitless experience, she sold Asian remedies for colds, lumbagos, sterility, iron and magnesium deficiency, she sold Indian cloth and jewels, Turkish carpets, they'd known each other for years, she trusted her. So I let her smear it over my prick, it had to be rubbed in for a long time to ensure that it penetrated the skin. Louise had a funny smile on her face that worried me, I let her proceed, dazedly watching my own mutilation, there was a faint smell of camphor, curcuma and centaury. In less than five minutes an anaesthetizing chill took hold of my member; it moved up as far as my testicles, to the point where the scrotum joins the crotch. My cock felt like it was at the North Pole, it was as stiff and as hard as a frozen courgette. Louise was satisfied, she wiped her hands, put the tube on the bedside table and starting French kissing me again. She'd taken off her blouse and her turquoise silk bra, I was naked except for the scarf that was keeping my neck warm, I'd also rubbed eucalyptus oil onto my throat. Louise took me in her strong arms, her mouth nibbled at my ears, my eyelids, my nose, my lips, she took my rod in her hand and caressed her vulva with it. Her breathing was rapid and irregular, she was a volcano on an ice floe, she was raping me, her pussy was engulfing me. Well, that was the last time she was going to take advantage of my weakened state! I felt nothing whatsoever, it was as though she'd placed a prop on a john thomas flattened by embolism, all it was for me was a vision of my ossified, frozen dick steaming with liquid nitrogen of the sort you use on warts. I was hopping mad, I nurtured my anger as Louise, her hips heaving, reached her climax, her mouth open, eyes closed, a saint!

When she came back down to earth, she made a fuss of asking me how I was feeling, her hands confirmed that my bone was showing no signs of subsidence.

'My goodness, my little Hercules, you haven't followed in my footsteps yet, have you?'

She was just being polite, she didn't give a shit really, she snuggled up against me and within two minutes was fast asleep. While she snoozed my dick melted like an eskimo on a hotplate, a sort of accelerated decrepitude, its skin was covered in reddish blotches and blistered in places. I wondered whether that poxy balm had had the same effect inside Louise's cunt. I gently disengaged myself from her, opened the window onto the garden and chucked the tube of balm out into the night, over my hedge, into the lane that runs along the prison wall. It landed in the rubble of the riot. I got dressed, went down the stairs on my wobbly legs, short of breath, poured myself a glass of brandy and sat down on the sofa with a modern edition of *Titus Andronicus*. I'd calmed down by the time I got to the end of Act I, where Titus refuses to give a decent burial to one of his sons, who he has just stabbed to death. But then Louise arrived, wrapped in the bedcover, her hair dishevelled, smiling.

'Did you put the balm away, Henry?'

'I threw it out.'

'What do you mean you threw it out?! That's not on, it cost me a fortune and . . .

'And it gives you blisters! I'm going to have hair loss and a dick as pink as a baboon's arse!'

'It's not my fault you're allergic to it. It didn't do anything to me.'

'I can see that! You were hoping for some more action, were you? You think I'm going to let myself be peeled like an onion?'

146

She went to the kitchen and started rummaging in the bin.
'I said I threw it out! You won't find it.'

She went upstairs to get dressed. When she returned to the living room she had her raincoat over her shoulders. She said she was off.

'Enjoy your book and good night!'

And bang! She slammed the door. Good luck and good riddance!

A dying dog week. The spectres return! Eleonore, Jane, Liz, Mary. Again they appear one by one in my bedroom. This time Eleonore stands on top of my bed, legs spread above my head, I see her sooty vulva, she pisses on me, her urine is like frothy milk.

'Remember the infinite contempt which I have always had for you, Henry, remember it when you fall to the ground.'

Liz has taken off her gauze veil. I can't make out her features, bone, flesh and cartilage are as one, her shapeless face is a fountain of bubbles of air and blood.

'You will remember your loving wife, won't you, Henry? When your heart stops pumping blood through your veins, you will again see the innocent woman you murdered.'

Mary has kept her dog's muzzle, she sniffs me with her wet snout, she paces around the bed like a crazed animal, her hands are padded and her fingers have claws.

'I'm cold,' she complains. 'I'm cold.'

But when Jane appears on her donkey with the schlong as long as my arm, she isn't alone, behind her, arms around her waist, is Louise, my God, Louise too! Her upper body trussed with copper wire that runs under her armpits, binding her breasts and penetrating her burnt flesh.

'Henry, my little old man. Your body will still be warm, it will be your last moment of consciousness, I shall emasculate you with my bare hands, I shall have your dick and your balls stuffed for an ornament on my kitchen shelf.

Ah, Louise, don't laugh like that, with your piercing laugh! Louise! Don't laugh! I beg you, don't . . . There's the account-ant, the one that was missing, in his navy blue suit, a diamond sewn into his red tie. He's at the foot of my bed, with one hand he strokes the donkey's nostrils, with the other he throws dice onto my bedcover, his hair is slicked back, he looks like a gambler in a casino.

'You're not real, Albert Exton,' I murmur.

He smiles shyly. He throws the dice again.

'I'm counting your days, Mr Blain. There aren't many left. They will be sleepless.'

I reach for the light switch, I knock over the bedside table, my back is rammed against the wall, my heels dig into the mattress, my heart convulses like a lobster in boiling water. It is Wednesday night, just a few hours after Louise walked out, slamming the door behind her. I switch on the radio, turn on the lights in the landing and in the hall downstairs, I walk around the house humming old love songs until dawn. The sky slowly grows pink and violet, the air is mild, birds twitter in the trees, the lawn is soft underfoot, dew wets my slippers. It's a sort of miracle every time, this morning silence when the garden awakes from its slumber. The sun pierces the mist, the sky has turned blue, not a cloud is to be seen. I piss into the hedge, the skin on my dick is flaking like pastry that's been baked too long, I'll have to rub walnut oil on it. I return to the kitchen to make myself a hearty breakfast. I am hungry, I eat well, I watch the morning news, I see the acrobatic mutineers on the roof, it is impressive, like a circus act. The phone rings half an hour later. I guess it'll be Louise wanting to apologize, but it is Helen asking if people from the HSP can come round that afternoon to visit their mutinous children. I then remember that on Sunday, when I was still feverish, I'd made a commitment to the HSP, in particular to Sandra and Helen Murray. And at present I am probably the most high-profile member of the HSP, because:

- I've been on television several times.
- I've declared my support for the mutineers.
- I've exposed the prison authorities' shady dealings.
- I'm being sued by the management.
- I've thrown open my garden and my house to the parents to enable them to speak with their children without being interrupted by the police. It's private property, the cops stay outside!
- The mothers are not charged entry; I supply them with tea and biscuits and participate in the struggle.

I say yes to Helen, she thanks me in her gentle, charming voice. I whistle all morning like a robin redbreast in springtime. The lawyers had organized the whole thing quite well, because a slew of newspaper, radio and TV journalists hovered around the group like wasps around a ham. I am on the toilet when the bell rings. On my throne, I had been taking my time on account of the large amount of medication I had swallowed over the past few days. I think about my nights with the ghosts, I was terrified by them. The strident bell gives me a start, I had been expecting them to arrive at three in the afternoon, it was only twenty to. In my haste I catch a corner of my shirt in my flies, that sort of thing always happens, always! I open the front door, I am machine-gunned by flashes, blinded by television camera lights. Sandra Murray is standing in front of me, in tears, her hair a mess, scarfless.

'Ah, Mr Blain, at last! Terrible news!'

The tears run down Mother Murray's face before gathering in the deep folds of skin created by her sorrowful grimace.

'The prosecution is going to ask for Nym and the others to

be given fifteen years. They want to make an example of them!'

Her face trembles like quince jelly, she sobs, blows her nose, coughs into a large checked handkerchief.

'The charges against them are ridiculous,' says Montfried over her shoulder. 'Insults, threats, attacking and injuring police officers, incitement to riot, disturbing the peace, revolting against the prison authorities, perverting the course of justice, vandalism, and damaging a listed government building.'

'A listed building!' I retort. '1,600 inmates crammed into a building made for 600!'

'Unless they surrender immediately,' gulps Mrs Murray. 'We'll have to convince them today!'

'We must remember that they've become the heroes of this prison revolt,' Montfried says. 'Another mutiny broke out yesterday in Shotts near Glasgow. If they give up now, the movement will come to an end.'

It's a real scrum at my front door, microphones jut into the air above our heads, I see Helen in the mêlée, crying, the poor thing. I'm almost blinded by the flashes. Ah, Louise! She's to my left, two yards away, in a spinach green suit and yellow blouse, she's playing at Trojan horses, she's going to march into my house as though nothing had happened, I stand aside to let the HSP members in, I turn the reporters away, Montfried insists I let the broadcast journalists in, I'm adamant.

'This is a private meeting,' I declare. 'There will be no journalists in my house.'

I manage to make out a few words in the ensuing brouhaha.

'A few words, Mr Blain! Please! For the BBC!' shouts one of them.

'For Talk Radio!' cries another.

'For Radio 5 Live!'

'For ITV! Please! Have you been sacked? What do you think about the libel action against you?'

It sounds like a fish market.

'I have no more fish to sell,' I say. 'I mean, I have nothing new to say. Yes, I have been sacked. Yes, the prison authorities are bringing a case against me. Which is an admission of guilt on their part. My only professional misconduct was to have exposed the state of the kitchens. I believe in justice. I have nothing more to say.'

Some of the rubbernecks break into applause. I humbly acknowledge them, I am dignified, responsible, I close the door, I should go into politics. My guests have already gone into the garden, Louise waits for me in the half-light of the hall, she throws her arms around me.

'Let's make up, Henry! We must help them, mustn't we? Those poor parents, it's so unfair. And ... and their children fighting for their dignity, fifteen years in jail!'

A little kiss, a long-tongues-entangled kiss, another little kiss, my hand is on her arse. We join the others, Louise offers them a drink, they look like they're at a wake. Of the two crying women I choose Helen, I take her in my protective arms, the arms of a mature, understanding man who seeks to provide comfort. She presses her head against my sholder, she smells nice. I'd love to kiss her tender white neck, but now is not the time, Mrs MacMorris is giving me funny looks, and then there is Louise, who arrives with a tray full of beer, bottles of spirits and a steaming teapot.

'How are we going to persuade them to come down from that cursed roof?' storms Mr Lawrence.

'The thing is,' remarks Mr MacMorris, 'that it's great up there. I had an uncle who was a roofer, he used to allow me up on the roofs with him, my mother never knew, of course. I remember the euphoria you get up there, you're happy, you're on top of the world, you can see for miles, people in the street seem so small, the tiles spread out in a pink and orange carpet at your feet, it's so beautiful!'

'There isn't a single tile left on that bloody roof, and anyway, they were slates,' snorts Mrs Lawrence.

MacMorris blushes, he falls silent, adjusts his tie and asks for a cognac.

'They must have faith in our justice system. There are laws, the individual is protected,' insisted Montfried.

'I'm going to talk to them! A double whisky, please, Louise, to put some fire in my belly.'

Everyone takes some fire for their bellies and I watch my bottles empty. Mother Murray grabs the loudhailer and sets off the siren, which sounds like a fleet of fire engines attending a blaze at the airport, it lasts thirty seconds. The mutineers appear on the roof, they're all wearing black balaclavas, you can't tell who's who, with the exception of Scroop, whose muscular former boxer's frame gives him away even at this distance. They crouch on the ridge, like ravens waiting for misfortune. One of them speaks through the megaphone.

'Hi, Mam, hi, Helen, hello everybody. It's really nice of you to come and see us. Are you all right? We're fine up here!'

'It's Nym,' murmurs Sandra Murray.

She drains another glass of whisky. She raises the loudhailer to her lips.

'Hello, Nym, darling. Listen to me, Nym, listen well.'

She explains the situation, she tells them of the police and the prison officers' humiliation, the prosecution's determination, fifteen years! Mother Murray shouts and sputters into the loudhailer, it's deafening in the garden. The birds, the moles and the mice will probably leave and never come back. The seven are having a good time up there, they're rocking with laughter, they're like monkeys scratching their balls and eating bananas at the same time. Nym gets to his feet, he tells his mother she's wrong, the government's running scared, the movement is spreading across the country! Besides, the damage they've done will be the same whether they surrender today or tomorrow. It's a cheap deal they're offering, it's blackmail!

'What do we gain if we give in now? Did they tell you? Thirteen years instead of fifteen?'

'Shit! He's right,' murmurs Mr Lawrence.

Nym is beside himself. If he got eight months for stealing a bicycle, he says, for three weeks of mutiny he'd get life! Another prisoner takes the megaphone, his voice is deep, his tone more measured.

'They treat us like animals, but they forget that men are capable of revolt. The prison service, the Home Office, and the Prime Minister are the only ones responsible for this. They light forest fires and then complain when the trees burn!'

'That's our Jason,' chorus Mr and Mrs Lawrence. 'What a voice!'

I go back into the house to get my binoculars, I want to try and identify them. Louise follows me into the living room-cum-study, she wants to know if I have any more alcohol, the bottles of spirits are already empty. We go into the kitchen, from under the sink I take out a bottle of brandy and a bottle of whisky.

'One last round and then I'm putting them away again. This is costing me a fortune.'

Louise clasps me in her arms, her eyes are shining, she's a bit tipsy, she mumbles that she's got things to tell me, she chuckles, she says something about Japanese techniques of strangulation that heighten the pleasure of an orgasm.

'It's what a hanged man feels, it has to do with carbon dioxide affecting the nerve cells, but you need to have a very light touch, got that, my hero?'

I get nothing, a shiver runs down my spine. I open the

brandy and have a swig, I must get back to the others, History is moving on.

I can make them out very clearly with my binoculars, they aren't wearing balaclavas, their faces are covered in soot. Mr Lawrence grabs the loudhailer, he greets the men one by one.

'Hello, Jason. Hello, Glyn. Hello, Nym, Fred, Paul, Dipack, George, hello! Why are you wearing those masks? I can't recognize any of you!'

'Morning, Dad. We aren't guests on some TV documentary, you know, we're on stage here, we're acting in the theatre of the world! We're taking risks! We're all wearing masks because we've each got a role to play. We're the rebels of Strangeways!'

'Didn't I tell you!' exclaims MacMorris. 'It's that buzz you get when you're up on a roof.'

Montfried asks for the loudhailer. I see Mother Murray joining her hands in prayer and stretching them up towards the prison rooftops.

'Gentlemen, I beg you! It's all very well to revolt, but you must also know when it is time to end your uprising. Your cause is just. This is recognized by . . .'

Jason has climbed up onto George's shoulders, he places his palms on the old boxer's shoulders again, there we go, he lifts himself up, his back, his behind, his legs go up in the air, he finds his balance, his feet pointing at the sky, we all fall silent. Montfried is disconcerted, his voice hesitant now.

'I'm your lawyer . . . Now is the time to start fighting on the legal front . . . We'll get you an amnesty.'

Another prisoner takes the megaphone. It looks like Fred Fluehler, I think he was wearing those overalls when I saw him on Sunday.

'In your dreams, lawyer! We're not government ministers, you know. Not even MPs. We're mere sailors aboard a ship on course for catastrophe!'

'It's Fluehler,' I cry out. 'The man who murdered his wife.'

'You know him?' asks Helen.

'I can see him clearly with my binoculars. Here, have a look.'

Jason is now sitting on George's shoulders. Two others, probably Glyn and Paul, are playing leapfrog on a chimney stack, their game gets faster and faster. We're flabbergasted.

'You won't gain anything by staying up there,' shouts an irritated Montfried.

'We know what we've got! We've got a hundred square yards here, at a height of 120 feet. We breathe, we eat, we sleep as free men, but our liberty is under threat every second. If we come down, your crooked justice will swallow us up and we'll be buried in some dungeon somewhere. "What shall we do? Let us, that have our tongues, plot some deuce of further misery, to make us wonder'd at in time to come." '

'Wait a minute,' I say to myself. 'Did I hear that right? That's . . . that's from *Titus Andronicus*! Act III!'

Louise, Helen, Mother Murray, Montfried and the others turn towards me. They look at me as if I had two heads. I mutter excuses, Sandra Murray shrugs, snatches the loudhailer from the lawyer and starts haranguing the mutineers, telling them they're at the peak of their glory, living dead . . .

'Living legends, Sandra, living legends,' Louise cuts in.

'That's what I said, they're living legends, yeah, more famous than the Beatles were when I was young, more popular than Princess Diana. Your fame will protect you, you've got to come down. My God! My God!'

Jason has climbed down along a wooden beam, he's at the gutter, he spreads his arms to form a cross, he jumps into the void, slowly, like a majestic bird taking flight. Screams rise up from the garden. Mrs Lawrence collapses unconscious into Louise's arms, Helen makes piercing little noises like a weasel caught in a trap, police sirens rend the air.

'Hello, Mam. Hello, Dad! Hello, my friends. The show goes on. No surrender!'

Jason's head appears above my treetops, level with the windows on the second floor of the prison, perhaps he's levitating.

'The nets!' exclaims Helen. 'He jumped into the nets!'

I run to the end of the garden, weave through the trees, I see him just fifteen yards away, he's laughing like a madman. Twenty police officers in riot gear await him in the lane, they stand amidst the rubble and burnt wood. Jason calls them dwarves, sneaks, shitbags, smelly foreskins, ponces, he moves around the net like a tightrope walker, he walks towards the prison wall, they point their tear gas launchers at him as if he were a nuclear threat. Jason puts his fingers to his mouth and whistles three times like a god of the wind; the rope tied around his waist tightens, he places his feet on the wall and begins his ascent, hauled up by his buddies.

'Give yourself up!' shout the policemen. 'You're surrounded! Don't move!'

Jason sniggers. Half-way up he turns around, his face towards the ground, his body perpendicular to the wall.

'Oh venal world, forgetful of death, we poor renegades shall reinvent you! Hello, Mam, hello Dad, my old friends, I love you, bye!'

I almost shout: 'Bravo, Jason! We're all with you!' but the cops are on the other side of my fence. He whistles again three times, then finishes his climb almost at a run, wings on his heels. Mrs Lawrence is revived, she's very pale, slumped on a garden chair. Her lips tremble, her lipstick is smudged, her husband administers a glass of brandy, he whispers noisily to her.

'Our son is a hero! A hero, woman, do you hear? Our Jason! I've never been so proud.'

I express regret that his exploits had not been filmed from my garden. Montfried turns to me.

'I did ask you to let the TV reporters in, did I not, Mr Blain?'

'Didn't you hear what our rebels said?' interrupts Louise. 'This is not some TV documentary, it's the theatre of the world we're dealing with here, and that's serious business. I'm going to write about it, I am, in the *Anglican Tribune*, I'm going to tell the truth about all this.'

'She's right,' says Helen. 'They're not fighting just to get on the telly. In any case, there are cameras all over the roofs of Strangeways.'

I'm vexed. I suggest another drink by way of diversion. We're all a little tipsy, we admit that that we'd been attempting the impossible.

'We have to give them time to think,' concludes Helen. 'The more we tell them to come down, the more stubborn they'll be.'

I lead my little tribe into the hall, I tell them my house is open night and day. Helen gives me a little smile, they thank me for my devotion to the cause. I open the front door, again we're blinded by flashes, assailed by questions. Louise whispers in my ear.

'Shut the door, Henry. Quickly!'

A man has marched up to me, I hadn't noticed him. He grabs my forearm in his iron fist.

'Hello, Mr Blain.'

I jump, it's Peter Bushy, my truck-driving neighbour, stocky brute, husband of Mary. He blows smoke from his cigarillo in my face. His look is piercing under his sailor's cap, he frightens me with his earring and his gypsy moustache. This April has been exceptionally warm and his feet stink, the stench mingles with the pong of his armpits. He smiles, he's a dangerous loony, he wouldn't dare strike me in front of the cameras, would he?

'Listen, matey, I want to say sorry for throwing you out the other day. I like what you said on the telly, and you're doing a good job with the support group. In Leeds, my boy is one of the leaders of the mutiny. The bastards are getting worried, aren't they, Mr Blain? We mustn't give in now, eh?'

'I'm really happy, Mr Bushy, that there's no hard feeling between us. The fight is right!'

He still has my hand in his vice-like grip.

'Can I join the HSP?'

'Of course you can! Just have a chat with the lawyer, that's the man in the grey suit talking to the journalists. You're very welcome, Mr Bushy!'

He releases me, he walks over to Montfried. Poor Peter Bushy, I stifle the manic laughter that is trying to escape from my mouth. Louise is waiting in the hall. I shut and lock the door, I lean against the wall, I hold my stomach, I almost die with laughter.

Chapter IX

Louise's body was found in the armaments factory on Sunday afternoon by a homeless man looking for a place to spend the night. His dribbling boxer dog must have sniffed her out, because the body was hidden under cables and coils of copper wire. I don't have a car, I never took the test. I lived on boats, and when I was eventually grounded I only had a few minutes to go to get to the prison. I take the train whenever I visit Mother in Liverpool. I couldn't carry Louise from the factory to the house. Five years ago I might still have had the strength, but anyway I could hardly walk through the estate – hello, dear neighbours, lovely day – with a corpse over my shoulder. I would've liked to have buried her in the garden, with the others, the trees and the flowers would have made for a lovely resting place. My cellar is my compost heap, my geological platform, I'm not cultivating virgin land, my garden is an historical and even archaeological area, it's my personal site, wherein lie loves, wars, martyrs, missing folk. But I had to leave Louise where she lay. The tramp went and told the police and they got there half-an-hour later. It was mentioned on the news that evening, and the *Anglican Tribune* paid homage to its intrepid reporter over six columns.

Louise wrote her last article about Strangeways on Saturday

21 April. It was spread over half the front and half the back page of the paper of which she was so proud. Three photos accompanied her text: one taken from the top floor of the armaments factory at the height of the mutiny – the sky was streaked with plumes of black smoke, thin silhouettes the shape of dried twigs gesticulated on the roofs; another taken from my room when the mutineers were flooding the street with their paper flowers; and finally one showing the founding members of HSP posing outside their office under a banner that read: HUMAN DIGNITY EVERYWHERE! The three lawyers are there, Montfried holds his hat over his chest. The article tells the story of the mutiny in great detail and tries to determine the significance, it speaks of Henry Blain as the kingpin of the movement, my stunning revelations were proof of the justness of the cause. 'Institutions today,' she wrote, 'whether they be schools, hospitals or prisons, are all too often seen by those in senior positions as an opportunity to line their own pockets.' I found the point well put, even if it had been made many times before, and not just in recent years. Besides, as old Durrell – the sensitive screw who was destroying his sinuses with lavender oil, the one they call Slow Bud – likes to say: 'Just be patient and the worst will happen,' which always had the effect of extinguishing the last glint of intelligence in his colleagues' eyes. Louise finished her piece by giving a lively description of the cheeky liberating escapades of Jason and his mates. She concluded: 'It is the theatre of a joyful apocalypse which, in this shameful world, still has faith in man.' Bravo, Louise! I won't raise my glass to your health, it's a bit late for that, but to your talent! You should've been writing for a national newspaper, cheers!

Louise had turned up on Saturday morning minus her aquarium-glass spectacles, she was wearing contact lenses, which showed me the real size of the green eyes in her unobstructed, smiling face. She had that day's *Anglican*

Tribune under her arm. I read her article attentively, we talked about the photos, we recalled our meeting in the armaments factory. Taking pictures from there was a stroke of genius. We decided to make a pilgrimage to the factory that afternoon to enjoy the lovely, sunny weather. And what a pilgrimage it was! Not one for quiet contemplation, for in a matter of days Louise had become an erotomaniac. On Thursday she'd urged me, during our frolics, to grip her throat at the carotid. On Friday morning, just after we woke up, she was choking herself, her cheeks were crimson, she gurgled in a strangled voice:

'Henry, Henry, that wasn't a mere orgasm, it was divine, it was cosmological, it was intergalactic! That article in *Weird Asia* was spot on!'

I'd never heard of the magazine. I looked at my trembling hands, I told her I'd prefer to touch her shoulders, her breasts, her waist, her bum, at the moment of ecstasy rather than having to pummel her neck. Louise didn't realize how intoxicating it would be for me to gently tighten my grip on her tender, warm throat, tighten it, tighten it, to feel her life slipping away in a few slow jolts, in the exhalation of an acid odour, puff! A bird flies up into the sky from between my hands! No, Louise! don't tempt me! She replied that she didn't care about my caresses, the partial asphyxiation of the lungs, the lack of oxygen going to the head increased the effect tenfold, it was like the 'sound of water dripping into the stoup of a deserted Romanesque crypt'. I must have looked completely dazed for her to laugh the way she did. I got annoyed.

'Next time I'll just keep my hands in my pockets!'

'Go ahead, I'll be fine on my own, I don't need you!'

I now looked on her as something worse than a stranger. We got up and got dressed, but didn't speak. Louise went off to her paper, I went to work in the garden. I planned to clear the rest of the debris, to give the hedge its spring trim, to prune the trees and the rose bushes, put some Bordeaux mixture around the trees and work the soil to prepare it for the new lawn I planned to sow in June. My garden would no longer be a hobby that I turned to when I got home from my kitchens, it would be my destiny, I would be an unemployed person who gardened, my deceased would see even more flowers, perhaps then they would stop haunting my nights.

That Saturday afternoon, Louise and I go hand in hand to the armaments factory. The sky is an intense blue, the birds are chirping in the gardens, only two mutineers, daubed in soot, naked from the waist up, stride up and down the ridge of the prison roof, like the queen's guard in front of Buckingham Palace. Thanks to her contact lenses, Louise no longer had to hunch her shoulders to scan the horizon through a glass screen. She carries her head more elegantly, she looks all around her, she blinks like a blind person who's just recovered her sight. We go past the north wall of the gaol, workers are replacing the heavy sliding door that was dynamited the first day of the riot. We step over a low wall of crumbling bricks, cross a small yard of gravel and weeds and enter the factory through a broken window. Sparrows circle under the glass roof, zigzagging between the metal girders. We go up to the top floor, to the place where Louise took her photos that first day. Visibility is perfect, the scale of the disaster all too apparent in the bright sunshine. Gutted, burnt roofs, chunks of wall knocked into the courtyards, all the furniture and the sanitary facilities seem to have been sucked out through the smashed windows. The prison is like the factory we are in, it's in ruins, hollowed out like an empty eggshell. Unfortunately, we can't see the block still held by the mutineers from here.

Louise wishes she'd taken her camera, she kisses me voraciously as though to make up for this. We venture onto the walkways in the nave, they shake, rattle and creak. The birds have flown out through the glass roof, two thirds of which is destroyed. Luckily, I'm wearing my tennis shoes, as an ex-sailor I'm steady on my feet. I hold Louise's hand, we wander from floor to floor, through a labyrinth of walkways cluttered with metal casing, generators, lockers, we pass under huge frames from which hang chains and pulleys, we pass work-benches, machine tools, lathes, all abandoned as though there had been a sudden exodus after orders had been given to evacuate the building. There's a pungent odour of rusting metal mixed with the acrid smell of overheated, burnt-out electric motors. I point out some nose cones and empty shells and bullets piled up at the foot of a crimping machine. I think I can also make out bits of machine guns and mortars.

'Weapons factory or no weapons factory, war is inside all of us, like the air we breathe, isn't it, Henry? Life has become so difficult, we're consumed by a sort of unspoken civil war, each of us silently fights his pathetic fight like a lost soldier, barbarity is never far away.'

I find no reply to Louise's philosophizing. We climb down a steep ladder, I go first, her black stockinged legs are just before my eyes. I slip my hand under her dress, I stroke her thigh, she says I never miss a trick. I'm not sure why we wander so obstinately among these ruins – at each turn Louise devours my mouth – we go round and round in circles as though trying to find a clearing to have a picnic. We end up in a narrow workshop. Louise sits on a workbench, she draws me towards her, her tongue runs over my neck, she pulls her skirt up around her waist, offers her breasts to me like warm fruit, and rubs her body against mine, stroking my quivering dick with a velvet hand. I have memories of this place; I throw her back onto the long table, her head next to a vice, I have an erection like a young stallion. Her legs wind around me, she grips me between her flabby thighs, I bathe in her creamy warmth, her ankles dig into my waist. I want to go on being as hard as a stallion for the next three hundred years – that wouldn't be long enough for me – but I know that in just a few years all I'll have between my legs is a mushy meringue whose only use will be to piss every hour. I think of Jane, of Liz, of Mary. I was talking aloud to Jane: 'Ah! Your white body, your adolescent breasts, here, in this place that looks like the end of the world!'

'Don't worry about me, Henry. I'm all right. It's your world that's going to pass away with your old carcass!'

And she filled the factory with her sniggers, the sneering, mocking witch.

'I'll be a great lady while you'll be pushing up the daisies in your back garden, Henry!'

'Stop, Jane! Stop!'

'Go on, darling, go on!'

Louise brings me back down to earth. I see on her neck a thin, silk cord with a slipknot, she's holding it in her hand, she pulls, she's trying to choke herself.

'Go on, Henry, go on!'

She can't manage it on her own, her hand is at too much of an angle. In despair she places the rope between my teeth. I pull with my head, my jaws clenched, the knot now slips wonderfully.

'Henry! Henry! Henr'ry! Hen . . .'

I work my Louise like a furious donkey, I bray, I bray wildly, I champ at the bit between my teeth, I pull harder. The movement of my head is uncoordinated, I use all the strength of my neck as though I wanted to break free from my tether, my back is arched, I'm in rut, Louise! I cry through my nostrils. Your trembling hands try to tear at my face, my eyes, your twisted fingers scratch me and draw blood, but I rear up,

I stand on my powerful back legs, I throw back my roaring head, I am the mad donkey that brays like a woodcutter's saw slicing through an oak, I wake the dead, ah, Louise! What hard work this is, the threads of the rope get between my teeth like strands of chicken breast, I'll snap the reins, smash the halter, tear the bridle, I rear up again, I draw myself up to my full height, a giant, I am your furious donkey, I bray one last time, I open my jaws, I release the silk rope, I hear a dull thump. Louise's head falls back onto the workbench, she has a fixed look on her face, her eyes bulge, her face is brick red, her tongue lies at the bottom of her throat, her neck is blue. Louise has been hanged from the teeth of a donkey.

On Friday morning, the day before the unfortunate pilgrimage to the armaments factory, I am in the garden doing some hoeing when the doorbell rings. I'm not expecting anyone. It's Helen and Mother Murray, on their own. I must look surprised, Helen puts a finger to her lips.

'Sssh! we've come on the quiet, Mam and me, it's not official. Can we come in?'

'We just wanted a quick chat,' croaks Mother Murray.

I lead them to the living-cum-dining room. I'm in my wellies and apron, I ask them to excuse my appearance. Sandra Murray is holding a large green rucksack from which she pulls out the loudhailer and a bottle of whisky.

'Did you watch the telly yesterday?'

'No, I didn't?'

'They showed Jason jumping into the nets, and they showed him climbing back up the wall . . . and when they were talking to us from up there, covered in soot . . . and what the authorities said afterwards: "The mutineers are able to parade on the rooftops because in this country the police are non-violent and are prepared to wait 'patiently' for them to see reason . . . they may well be poets or acrobats, but they are also people who have committed crimes and who are serving sentences for these crimes . . . we are all equal before the law . . . the mutiny is illegal . . . no one will escape justice! No one can expect a pardon after participating in disturbances as serious as these!" It's all over, Mr Blain, it's going to be terrible, they're going to send them all over the country, they'll be abused in some high security wing somewhere, they'll be forgotten, I won't see my Nym again for ten years, they'll break him, they'll break them all!'

'Do you believe in the justice system, Henry?' asks Helen.

'Where is the justice in this, Helen?' I ask heatedly. 'Just where is the justice? It's in the hands of the people with power, and they do what they like with it! We're all guilty in some way, but only the truly guilty know this . . . I believe in the wrath of ghosts as I draw near to my death!'

'Would the night were come!
Till then sit still, my soul: foul deeds will rise,
Though all the earth o'erwhelm them, to men's eyes.'

I declaim.

They look terror-stricken, I've troubled them. I knock back my glass of whisky.

'Forget all that,' I say. 'I'm just having a bad day. What can I do for you?'

Mother Murray pulls herself together, she explains that she's come to talk to her son alone, not in the middle of a battle as though he were a warlord ready to fight to the death, she wants to try one last time to persuade him to come down. She sobs, her nose and chin turn red, her quince jelly quivers. I look down at my muddy wellies.

'You might end up on the telly,' I point out. 'The cameras are switched on all the time, the other members of the HSP might find out, it could split the group.'

Too bad, too bad, too bad! She asks me, as an active

member of the committee, if I'd be prepared to overlook this act of a loving mother. I look at her daughter Helen, with a sweet little face she has! And a stunning body just waiting to be caressed! Again she's wearing a miniskirt, a pullover pulled down tightly over her little round breasts, her cat's eyes beseech me, her cherry lips smell of fruit. I draw myself up, weary.

'Very well, Mrs Murray, after all . . .'

They leap to their feet, I open my arms, I press them to my heart, I feel Helen's thigh against my own, I breathe in her hair, I place a kiss on her head. I offer to stay inside the house, it's better if Nym doesn't see me. Mother Murray smiles.

'Ah, Mr Blain! You're so tactful.'

I remove my wellies and my apron and settle down on the sofa. I pick a volume of Shakespeare at random from my shelves, volume two of a prestigious 1703 edition, it contains *Macbeth*, *King Lear* and *Hamlet*. I can see them out there in the garden, Sandra Murray has switched on the loudhailer but hasn't set off the siren. She whispers into the megaphone, her voice won't carry more than a hundred yards.

'Nym, son, can you hear me? Nym, it's your Mother! Talk to me, Nym! What are you up to? Are you there?'

There is silence on the rooftops, they're having a siesta, they're playing cards, or maybe they've surrendered. Normally there are two of them keeping watch day and night. Sandra Murray turns anxiously towards her daughter. She looks back up at Strangeways.

'Nym! It's your mother, talk to me!'

I try to concentrate on *Hamlet*, which I've opened on Act III. I read: 'I must be cruel, only to be kind. Thus bad things and worse remains behind.' It's the son speaking to his mother; poor Mother Murray, if she read that . . . Nym finally responds.

'Hello, Mam!'

167

He says this is much better than in the visiting room, you get a lot more visits, they're out in the fresh air, you can say what you want, those lousy screws aren't listening in, it's the whole world, they're as alone as they would be if they were sitting in their kitchen having homemade plum pudding. Sandra explains that she's come off her own bat, this isn't a HSP thing now, if Nym doesn't want to come down for the HSP, then she wants him to come down for her, she'd die to think of him spending the next fifteen years in some dark and dank fortress in deepest Scotland, she'd never see him again, he'd be separated from his mates, mistreated, humiliated, broken like a piece of porcelain, and he only had another five months to serve in Strangeways.

'It's mad, isn't it, Nym?'

The son doesn't reply. Through the French windows I can only see part of the prison roof. I can only suppose that Nym is conferring with his fellow mutineers.

'Do you remember?' she murmurs, for the entire estate to hear. 'Do you remember the day I came to get you from school and I forgot to bring your little fire engine like I promised, you were in such a sulk, you had a big long face on you, the teacher tried to cheer you up, as well as trying to chat me up, after a couple of minutes he'd forgotten you and was concentrating on me, you kicked him in the shin, he was holding his leg in both hands, he was white as a sheet, hopping around on one foot, like a one-legged chicken. "She's not your mam, she's mine!" you told him. Remember that, Nym? And do you remember the night your dad was really ill, there was snow and it was foggy. I was driving, we were taking him to the hospital, four hours on the road, he was knocked senseless with morphine, you kept talking, about your toys, your friends, about your girlfriend, the cute little nine-year-old next door, you kept talking to me really calmly as though you wanted to reassure me and not let me fall asleep at the wheel, remember that, Nym?'

Nym remembers it all perfectly well, but he doesn't see what it's got to do with this battle they're having with that bitch Thatcher, who is selling England off to the highest bidder.

'They've even flogged the cemeteries in London, Mam! She's already thrown the poor out onto the street and now she's doing the same with the dead! That's what's happening in this country of ours, Mam!'

'Nym, Helen's just been sacked by her bank, they found out she was your sister, they accused her of professional misconduct. You see, Nym, they won't give in, you can't win, son, you'll lose everything.'

Mother Murray begins sobbing for the whole estate, I pity her. Helen wants to take the loudhailer.

'We still have a few hours of freedom!'

It's no longer Nym's voice, it could be Jason. I go out into the garden, instead of seven blackened faces, I see seven milk-white bums lined up along the roof. The one holding the loudhailer shouts into it.

'Good morning, UK!'

He pulls up his trousers.

'That wasn't aimed at you, Mrs Murray, we love you, we were mooning at those miserable bastards who want to lock us up for ever.'

'I'm begging you, lads! You can't win, you just can't win!'

She drops the loudhailer, her large body subsides, the slumps on my lawn, two steps away from the rhododendrons, she's crying her eyes out. Helen has knelt down beside her, she puts her slender arms around her, I really must find a pretext for inviting this beauty to dinner. The voice of Fred Fluehler accompanies Mother Murray's collapse.

'We defy augury: there's a special providence in the fall of a sparrow. If it be now, 'tis not to come; if it be not to come, it will be now; if it be not now, yet it will come: the readiness is all: since no man has aught of what he leaves, what is't to leave betimes?'

'Oh! Oh!' I shout. 'That's ... that's Hamlet!'

Helen turns her pretty, stupefied face to me, she looks horrified.

'Help me get her inside,' she says. 'We can put her on the sofa.'

Mother Murray no longer has a face, the place where it was is now an oedema of red flesh, eyeless, flooded with tears, it keeps croaking:

'You can't win, you just can't win!'

I didn't want to be on my own the evening after Louise was hanged. I left the armaments factory and walked by the badly lit warehouses, along the black canal that smells of sludge. I crossed the Fairfield estate, where the textile workers live, and arrived in Oak Street, at the end of which is Suzan Carlos Simson's pub. I wanted to sit and drink beer amidst the noisy Saturday night crowd. I pushed open the door and found myself in the middle of a crush of people. The room was so smoky I couldn't see the walls. I vainly sought a seat and had just taken up my position at the bar when I heard a shout behind me.

'Woooow! If it isn't the prison movement leader himself come back to his old watering hole!'

I jumped. Suzan took me in her arms and planted a kiss on each of my cheeks, greeting me as in the old days, before this mutiny business.

'Why did you say watering hole?' I ask, a little tense. 'I'm not a cow, after all.'

'I was only joking, Henry. Besides, I was thinking more of thirsty horses.'

'Horses don't drink beer either ...'

'You're your old self again, I see! It's great to see you again! I was reassured when I saw you make that statement on the telly. And now with your work on the support group . . . I sent you a cheque, you know! We had a whip-round among the customers. It came to 328 pounds.'

'That's great. A pint of Guinness, please.'

'This one's on me.'

I had to shake hands with at leasty thirty people who came up to say how much they admired my courage. I drank three pints as though they were mineral water, I felt relaxed. I drank two more and felt old and pathetic. Suzan found me a seat, and when the pub began to empty at around eleven o'clock, she came over to have a drink with me and chat about the future. Her volumnious red hair tumbled over her green velvet jacket.

'There isn't much of a future at my age, is there? I wouldn't mind being a grandfather, then I might be of some use. I could play the wise old man to my grandchildren, couldn't I, Suzan?'

'You'd need to become a father first. You'd better hurry up.'

'You're right, Suzan, we'd better get right down to it . . .'

'You old lech! With all the wives and mistresses you brought here, you'd think you could've produced something . . . Speaking of which, how's your Louise?'

'She's all right.'

'She's a believer, isn't she? I've read her articles, she writes really well, no waffle.'

I drink the remaining two thirds of my pint in one go, my shoulder touches Suzan's.

'My lease is running out, Suzan. Soon I'll have to vacate the premises, leave this old body I've lived in more or less happily for such a short time. Times goes on and on, and this breath that makes my chest rise and fall, expands my muscles, stirs my blood, lights up my eyes at the sight of a pretty woman like yourself, this breath will one of these days disappear into the air, pouf! One last contraction of the diaphragm, one last expulsion. Not even the wallpaper or the carpets will be recognizable in the premises that remain, the rooms will be empty and broken, open to the elements, ill winds will blow through them. Listen to me, Suzan, instead of looking over my shoulder to see whether Ulysses is collecting the empty glasses.'

'You're a bundle of laughs tonight, Blain.'

'Two minutes, Suzan, two minutes! I was never idle, never lazy, I don't think I used my time as if it was unlimited, like a rich bastard recklessly spending his cash, no, no, no, I was in a hurry! I was like the poor bugger who plays the lottery and wins three days in a palace somewhere in the Pacific. I drew the iodized air deep into my lungs, sank my teeth deep into the flesh of shellfish. I knew from the start it'd only last three days, one lifetime is not enough, I'm going to have to go, leave behind this old carcass. I'm on the third day, Suzan, it's midday, the sun is at its last zenith, I don't know if I have the strength to last until it sets.'

'Is it your sacking that's put you in this state? I told you before, I'd be very happy to have you in the kitchen here. I'll have a chat with my bookkeeper about it. You could start on the first of May, if you like.'

She makes a little sign to Ulysses at the bar, he brings me another pint. I raise it to my lips, I look at its creamy head, I'd like to dive into it, I drink to drown myself. I put down the glass, I sway, I sense Suzan standing up, then a curtain comes down, I conk out on the bench.

I woke up on my sofa at midday on Sunday, a scrawled note from Suzan said she'd found the house keys in my jacket pocket and had brought me home in Ulysses' car. Mother phoned in the afternoon, she'd seen more moving scenes on the news – the tearful mother begging her mutinous son to give himself up. She supposed it had taken place in my garden, the camera had been looking down on the scene from very high, Mrs Murray had looked really small, like a broken egg on the ground, her tearful face lifted toward the sky; it was obvious she was talking to her son, you could clearly hear the prisoners' responses. Mam had thought she recognized the house, she had thought she might be able to see me next to that poor woman, who so lacked authority. The head of the prison warders' union had been interviewed, he said the mutineers had proved that they were lost souls because only lost souls could fail to heed such prayers from a sorrowful mother. Mam asked me if I'd found myself a lawyer.

'And when are you going to go fishing at Prince's Dock? Mr Shallow says the Mersey's teeming at the moment, you could cook me some fresh fish, it'd do you good, Henry, a weekend at home. You could bring your Louise along ... Are you going to get married?'

'We're not planning anything at the moment, Mam ... Things have cooled down a bit between us.'

'That doesn't sound at all good, son. But come on your own, then. They're always talking about you at the widows' club. They all support your cause, Mrs Page and Mrs Overdone are dying to meet you. You know, Henry, I reckon you should go into politics, you come across really well on the telly. It's about time our family got a bit of respect!'

Mother lives in a terraced house in Birkenhead, it smells of cat piss and mutton stew that's gone off. I'm so allergic to the hairs of her three Persian cats that I almost sneeze my brains out every time I go there. She's obsessed with saving money despite the fact that she has a widow's pension, a nurse's pension, and another one on account of having lost her husband in the war. On top of that, she owns the house she lives in. She never switches the lights on until it's completely dark, but operates by the light from the television screen, which means that most of the time the place looks like somebody's just died. The stuffed birds on the walls cast grotesque shadows, but Mam won't change a thing. My father was a renowned taxidermist, and when he was killed by a shell on a French beach during the landings she took the best of the birds in his workshop and decorated the whole house with them. An owl stares at you when you're sitting on the bowl in the bog. I made a vague promise to come and see her some weekend in May and we said goodbye; she put down the phone before me.

On the news that evening I heard about Louise's death, the discovery of her body in the disused armaments factory. Her views on the Strangeways mutiny were believed to be a factor, the case was attracting a lot of interest. The phone kept ringing. I disconnected it, I spoke to no one. I didn't plan on sleeping, but somehow, around two in the morning, I ended up dozing on the sofa, having polished off a bottle of sherry. The doorbell woke me on Monday morning at nine o'clock. It rang and rang, I got up, everything was pitching in my living-cum-dining room, the bones in my skull felt like they were encrusted with sea urchins. I fixed my tie and my trousers and dragged myself to the door. At the door, I found myself face to face with two giants in beige raincoats who blocked the horizon. One of them raised his felt hat by way of greeting, the other showed me his police ID, they asked if they could come in. I led them to the study.

No, I'm sorry. I've no idea why they're here.

No, my God! I didn't know that Louise had been murdered, strangled probably, the post mortem suggested the death had occurred late on Saturday afternoon, Jesus!, I'm flabbergasted, my eyes are misty with tears.

No! We hadn't arranged to meet on Sunday despite our budding relationship.

No! I didn't think it strange that she hadn't contacted me. My God! It's horrible! I take out my handkerchief, I blow my nose noisily.

No! I didn't know of any enemies she might've had, she was a woman who gave a lot of herself. She was sincere, people liked her.

No! I'd no idea what she might have been doing in the factory.

No! I didn't know what she had planned to do on Saturday evening. I dry my eyes. I'm sorry!

'You were seen together in the estate on Saturday afternoon, you were walking arm in arm. Isn't it odd that you didn't try to get in touch with her on Sunday? There was no message from you on her answering machine. Yet you were lovers . . . Fate would seem to be against you, Mr Blain. Two wives disappear, a girlfriend murdered . . .'

I cry, I sniff, I dab at my eyes, I sigh, I blow my nose, I'm dumbfounded, I'm dazed. Their backsides are like anchors sinking to the depths of my tired armchairs. The crotches of their trousers are too tight, their danglers are on display, one on each side of the stitching, they breathe heavily, their backs are arched, their elbows screwed to their thighs.

I head for the kitchen to get a can of beer. I down it greedily to calm my hangover. I have the giggles, I splutter, I bury my face in a clean cloth, I bite the palm of my hand till it bleeds, I want to burst out laughing. The older of the policemen, the one wearing the felt hat, gives me a start, he's standing behind me in the doorway. I take another sip of beer, I almost choke myself, I cough, which hides the laughter that's taking hold of me, I bury my face again in the cloth. Inspector what's-his-name is nearly bald, his eyelashes are almost non-existent, he has a salt-and-pepper moustache, he thinks I'm having breathing problems brought on by the terrible news. He speaks gently to me, they won't keep me any longer, he's sorry. I pull myself together and accompany them to the front door. I manage to say, through gritted teeth:

'I hope you find the bastard who did it!'

They have some good leads, they assure me. I close the door behind them, I can't even stand up any more, I've got cramps in my stomach. The bell rings again, it's the baldy one.

'Sorry, Mr Blain,' he mumbles. 'Just one more question. Where were you on Saturday evening?'

'Er . . . I was with Suzan Carlos Simson, I spent the evening in her pub. It's on Oak Street.'

They say goodbye again, off they go. The giggles set in, my ribcage aches, I fall like a shrimp net onto the tiles in the hallway. I can't see properly, I laugh out all the tears in my body, I want to bray, I must turn on the lights.

I join them late in the morning on Tuesday, 24 April.

'All hail, rebels! Hail, heroes of a just cause! Hail, the unsubdued of this putrid society! Solidarity! Solidarity!'

'Welcome!' they reply. 'Welcome, cook of misfortune! Welcome to the club of the condemned.'

I too am on the roof, the roof of my house, standing on the slope, holding the megaphone Sandra and Helen Murray left behind after Friday's debacle. I was in the attic gathering up maggots, line and hooks to go fishing. I was planning on going to see Mother at the weekend, when I heard them shouting. The loudhailer was rammed between two rafters, they were perched on a chimney stack and were speaking as though on a stage, passing the megaphone back and forth. I open the skylight, put the stepladder in place and thrust my upper body out into the air. I recognize Jason's voice.

'Hang out our banners on the outward walls; the cry is still

"They come", our castle's strength will laugh a siege to scorn:
Here let them lie till famine and the ague eat them up.'

I immediately recognized the companion of all my infamies,
it was as though a hornet has stung me in the bum. I race to
the living room-cum-study, pick up the 1786 edition of
Macbeth, the one with the honey-coloured leather binding and
run back up the stairs, four steps at a time. I'm still as vigorous
as a young man. I climb back onto the roof and listen to their
theatre of insurrection. It is the Indian's turn to speak, in his
effeminate, strongly accented voice.

Dipack Kappoor: The queen, my lord, is dead.
Jason: She should have died hereafter;
         There would have been a time for such a word.
         Tomorrow, and tomorrow, and tomorrow,
         Creeps in this petty pace from day to day
         To the last syllable of recorded time,
         And all our yesterdays have lighted fools
         The way to dusty death.

Me: All hail, mutineers! Hail, insurgents! I greet you!

That stops them short. They look at me like they've just
spotted a fly in their crème caramel.

'Solidarity!' I shout. 'Solidarity with the men who won't give
in! With the heroes of a just cause!'

They ask me why I, Henry Blain, torturer of stomachs, am
rallying to their cause.

'I am not a torturer! I'm not going to get anything out of
this. Not only did I have to do my job in Strangeways with
very meagre means, but I did it artistically! I'm an artist,
comrades!'

Fluehler: And we're the bagpipes you play your nauseating
music on!

Me: Exactly, Fred! I'm a wind artist, you are my choir, my
symphony orchestra! I want all arseholes to be in tune, to
vibrate, to sing, to rumble, to thunder, to ring out! And now

they've gone and stopped me, and they make terrible accusations against me!

From my pocket I take the letter I received that morning and wave it at them.

'Look, this is an order to go and see a lawyer, a certain Edgar MacDuff, this is confirmation that the prison authorities are bringing a case against me. I have to go to see him in his office on 9 May at three o'clock. I have to bring my own lawyer with me!'

I see them bend double with laughter, they think it's a big joke.

'The world is not a serious place,' chuckles Nym. 'Come on up here! Come and join us!'

'But I'm already with you.'

'You still have a few storeys to climb, Blain.'

They're taking the mickey. I stand up on tip-toe, I stake my all, I want them to respect me. I open my book at scene v, Act V.

'I 'gin to be aweary of the Sun, and wish the estate o' the world were now undone. Ring the alarum-Bell! Blow, wind! Come, wrack! At least we'll die with harness on our back.'

Silence from up above. The seven sooty heads are conferring.

Jason: Thou comest to use thy tongue; thy story quickly.

Me: Gracious my lord, I should report that which I say I saw, but know not how to do it.

Jason: Well, say, sirs.

Me: As I did stand my watch upon the hill, I look'd toward Birnam, and anon, methought, the wood began to move.

Jason: Liar and slave!

Me: Let me endure your wrath, if't be not so. Within this three mile may you see it coming; I say, a moving grove.

Jason: If thou speak'st false, upon the next tree shalt thou hang alive, till famine cling thee.

I don't have time to reply, I feel her hand on my shoulder, light as a bird. She's there, mysteriously appeared from I know not where. I shiver, I feel oppressed, alone and lost. She's wearing stockings and a red blouse over a champagne-coloured bra. Her neck is marked with a scar, whose lips are yellow and blue, a bloody rope is embedded in her flesh. Louise places the end of the rope in my hand, I hold her by the bridle, she repeats in a hoarse voice:

'To bed, to bed! . . . Come, come, come, come . . . What's done cannot be undone. To bed, to bed, to bed!'

I release the rope, I shout into the megaphone.

'I have almost forgot the taste of fears. The time has been, my senses would have cool'd to hear a night-shriek; and my fell of hair would at a dismal treatise rouse and stir as life were in't. I have supp'd full with horrors. Direness, familiar to my slaughterous thoughts cannot once start me.'

Fluehler cuts in, half mocking, half angry.

'What are you up to Blain? You doing the play backwards? It's not you who says that, it's Jason. You're mucking the whole thing up. Pay attention!'

'But it *is* me! I'm the one under siege! "Why should I play the Roman fool, and die on mine own sword? Whiles I see lives, the gashes do better upon them." '

Louise is sweating blood, she moves away backwards, she looks at me as though I were already dead. The megaphone falls from my hands, I clutch the book to my chest. I stumble, I fall sprawling on to the roof, I slip, I slide, my foot catches in the gutter. My neck presses against a warm tile, the mutineers are calling to me, they're worried.

'You're too old to be walking around the roof, mate!' shouts Nym.

I get to my feet and crawl back up the slope on all fours. I sit astride the ridge of the roof, Nym continues to scold me.

'What are you getting on your high horse about, Blain? What cause are you fighting for?'

'I have lived long enough,' I snap back. '"My way of life is fall'n into the sear, the yellow leaf. And that which should accompany old age, as honour, love, obedience, troops of friends, I must not look to have. But, in their stead, curses, not loud but deep, mouth-honour, breath, which the poor heart would fain deny, and dare not." '

But no one can hear me. I no longer have the loudhailer, my voice is no more than a whimper. Jason's warm, powerful voice interrupts me.

' "Life's but a walking shadow, a poor player that struts and frets his hour upon the stage and then is heard no more. It is a tale told by an idiot, full of sound and fury, signifying nothing." '

That's it, I grab the loudhailer, I'm back on my feet, I find my balance.

'That's not true! "The mind I sway by and the heart I bear shall never sag with doubt nor shake with fear." Not true! I won't die! I will go unpunished!'

'Holy Virgin of Padua! God of mercy! What are you doing up there, howling like a wolf at full moon? Henry? Henry? What's going on?'

The tremulous voice comes from behind me, from street level. I turn slowly, Romeo is standing in the middle of the road, his arms are laden with pots; he's wearing his Sherlock Holmes cap and a brown velvet jacket over his gardening apron, he's got wellies on.

'Good Heavens! You'll break your back if you fall from up there. Come down, I'm begging you. My God! And I've brought you all this stuff to restore your Arcady.'

With his chin he gestures towards his old Austin estate, which is crammed with yet more pots. He stamps his heel on the tarmac.

'Come down at once! Come down, everyone's looking at you, Henry!'

I look around and see about twenty people standing in the street, looking up at me. I recognize the unemployed couple from the next street, pensioners returning to the estate with their shopping baskets, three bored teenagers who're always hanging about, on the lookout for their next round of petty crime. I spot Peter Bushy in his blue overalls stained with machine oil, cap pushed well back over his head, fists resting on his hips; he sucks nervously on his cigarillo, he looks disconcerted. Ten yards further along stand two people I don't recognize, they wear leather jackets, their elbows rest on the roof of their car, they look like detectives sent to monitor communications between the prisoners and myself.

'Blain, you old artist torturer!' hollers Fluehler. 'It's Fred here! You're all right, mate! You really are guilty! Guilty among the guilty, we all agree. But we reckon you're not cut out to be an actor. You don't have presence, and you fluff your lines! You're better on the telly, spilling the beans. Stick with Mrs Murray and the HSP, and stay on the ground floor, keep both feet on the ground!'

'He's already got one in the grave!' sneers the Malcolm boy, that little bastard of a thirteen-year-old who scrawls inanities on the walls, sticks chewing gum on doorbells and pours acid over the local cats.

I watch the blokes in leather jackets out of the corner of my eye. One of them is now sitting in the blue Rover, he's on the phone, he's making his report, I'm sure they're cops. I head nonchalantly for the skylight, my head spins, my legs are like jelly, my feet unsure. I lean, I bend, I wriggle, I find the rungs of the ladder. I descend slowly, but graze a forearm and a knee, the skin burns. There we go, I'm back in the attic. I hear Romeo's impatient finger on the doorbell. 'I'm coming, I'm coming!', I shout. I open the door.

'Jesus Christ! You're as white as a sheet. My poor Henry! It's all right, don't say anything! I know, I know, you're having a hard time of it!'

I whisper to him to leave the pots in the hall. I help him make space for them.

'Look at that!' he says. 'I'm spoiling you. An aeonium, a tillandsia and a beloperone guttata! And there're three azaleas and a pair of camellias in the car.'

I thank him half-heartedly.

'Romeo ... Louise told me I was going to die when we were up on the roof.'

Romeo makes the sign of the cross and excuses himself. He goes off to get the azaleas, I hear him muttering a prayer. He returns loaded like a packhorse, a strained smile on his thin face.

'The earth is warming up with this sun, now's the time to do your planting ...'

'I can't dig any more ...'

'Why's that? Have you got tendinitis? Low blood pressure? Your heart playing up?'

'The earth is haunted, Romeo. With every turn of the spade I disturb bones. The spectres are not pleased and ...'

Romeo pulls off his hat and raises his eyes to heaven. He moans and crosses himself twice. His snow-white hair is tousled, he stares at me as though he's examining the back of my skull through my pupils.

'I'd thump you if you were my son! The world began with a garden! Gardens honour the dead, they appease the living, the world will end in a garden!'

'In a prison, more like!'

'Oh, shut up! You need to get back to work. Do some hoeing, raking, pruning, planting, you'll see, it'll put new life into you ... I had my doubts about you, you know. But when I saw you making that statement on the telly, with your big cigar that made you look a bit weird, I could've hugged you. You were the voice of Truth! Forgive me for asking, but when is Louise's funeral?'

'I don't know, I don't know, they're having an inquest, they're looking for clues.'

Romeo won't have anything to eat or drink, he won't even sit down for five minutes. Elizabeth is with Charles, they're having their first yoga session. Romeo has to get back to the garden centre, he doesn't like leaving the Scottish twins on their own for too long. I thank him profusely, he says I must come round for dinner, he'll give me a call. He too makes his exit walking backwards, waving at me. He beeps his horn a few times as though he were marking the departure of a pair of newly-weds, the old horn squeals like a duck being throttled. I close and lock the door, I smear antiseptic over my forearms and knee, I sit down on the sofa with my 1786 edition and a glass of brandy. I wait, I don't know what I'm waiting for. I think and I wait. He's dreaming, that Romeo, with his garden! The police have not only surrounded the prison, they've circled my house and the estate. Soon it'll be the town and the country, then the whole planet. Their microphones and their cameras will be planted in our walls and their radars above our heads. I'm not deluding myself, it'll be done in the name of the Law even if they claim it's in the name of justice. But justice, with the exception of ghosts who come to terrorize us and make us suffer, will never be done! There's too much of a backlog. Even to judge from my case alone, the delay is considerable. Justice is on the menu, but what you get on your plate is their law, which cracks your teeth like the lentils I used to serve the lags. Ah, those inspired mutineers, the seven funambulists, munching the last biscuits from the warders' canteen! Three or four more days of turbulence and it'll be over. In a few weeks it'll all be forgotten, like the hiccoughs, like the wind in my treetops. Poor Mother Murray . . . I don't know what I'm going to cook tomorrow evening, a lamb dish, or maybe duck. I want it to be something delicate and refined, Helen's coming to dinner. I'm tired, one last glass of brandy. Cheers!